WIDOW'S TRAIL

A Frontier Romance

S. M. Revolinski

Copyright ©2017 by S. M. Revolinski
All Rights Reserved
No part of this document may be reproduced or transmitted in any form or by any means, electronic, mechanical, photocopying, recording, or otherwise without prior written permission of S. M. Revolinski.

Acknowledgments:
Many thanks go to Sheila Dunbar for her tireless effort, editing my work into this masterpiece.

The cover art was created using www.selftpubbookcovers.com. Book cover credit and thanks go to: SelfPubBookCovers.com/parkerclvs

ISBN: 9781790754151

CONTENTS

Chapter One 2
Chapter Two 7
Chapter Three 14
Chapter Four 22
Chapter Five 27
Chapter Six 36
Chapter Seven 44
Chapter Eight 57
Chapter Nine 64
Chapter Ten 71
Chapter Eleven 84
Chapter Twelve 92
Chapter Thirteen 97
Chapter Fourteen 107
Chapter Fifteen 115
Chapter Sixteen 122
Chapter Seventeen 127
About The Author 130
Free Sample of 'A Pirate's Wife For Me' 131

CHAPTER ONE

April 15, 1848
Cincinnati, Ohio

"I do," Gerturde Hengel proclaimed, just as her father had instructed.

After her seventeenth birthday, he had insisted she marry. She had nothing against being married. She had dreamt of having a loving husband and children. However, Cupid's arrow had never found her heart. Not only was her father unwilling to continue her support, Gertie was blocking the marriage of her younger sister. It was socially unacceptable for the younger sibling to marry first, and Ida had already accepted a marriage proposal. Their mother's remedy had been to locate Mr. Berg for Gertie to marry.

As her mind wandered, Gertie became aware of a sudden silence. The Preacher was staring at her; he nodded toward Peter. Gertie had missed the Preacher's announcement that they were now man and wife. She had missed his statement: "And now you may kiss the bride."

Gertie turned to her new husband. He was an inch shorter than her five and a half foot tall frame. She bent her knees ever so slightly to bring their noses to the same height. Peter Berg lifted her veil. She looked upon his round face and bushy black beard. She looked deeply into a man's eyes for the first time ever. He held her shoulders. She stood stock-still as he leaned forward and brushed his lips with hers.

Gertie did not move as he backed away—smiling. It was her first ever kiss on the lips, and it was not entirely unpleasant. Her mother had promised she would come to love her new husband—eventually. "He's a fine man from a solid German family," Gertie's mother had said. She had gone on to explain that his first wife had died in childbirth six months earlier. Being the ripe age of seventeen, Gertie would have to settle for an older, previously married man. Peter was twenty-three. The soon-to-be-married couple had been introduced and spoke briefly. There had been no long sighs or deep piercing looks. They had awkwardly held hands. Her father had slaughtered a pig for their hastily arranged engagement party. Gertie had danced with her new fiancé, Peter. And now, they were married—all within the short span of a week. Her life had become a foggy dream and she had no control over what would come next. Gertie's life was changing.

Tugging on her arm, Peter pivoted his bride to face the small gathering of family and friends. She forced herself to smile. He took a half step forward, and tugged her arm to pull her along beside him. Gertie remained rooted for a moment before taking her first step as man and wife. Arm in arm, the newlyweds slowly walked between the stained oak pews and outside, to the church rose garden.

They greeted their well-wishers. The men kissed the new Mrs. Berg on her cheek, and slipped coins and banknotes into the purse dangling from her wrist. Someone began playing a violin. Their previous dance had been a square-dance in her father's barnyard. This time, they danced a waltz. Gertie enjoyed having Peter's strong hands hold her. He held her very close against his chest. Her pulse raced; Gertie had never before been permitted to hold a man so close.

Maybe Mother is right and marriage won't be too bad at all, she thought to herself.

Gertie was beginning to enjoy being married.

The newlyweds ate, drank wine, and danced as the sun drifted into the west. Twilight settled and the men gathered around Peter to smoke cigars and drink whiskey. Gertie's mother pulled her aside.

"Dear, I need to tell you about tonight—your wedding night," she whispered into Gertie's ear. "Mr. Berg has been married before, and he will know what to do. You must simply lie still and let him have his way."

"What?" Gertie whispered back, though she knew exactly what her mother was referencing.

The Preacher interrupted, with Peter in tow. "It's time for me to give the newlyweds their private blessing," he said.

Peter took her arm and they followed the Preacher into the church. He closed the door. Gertie and Peter sat while he stood over them. The three held hands in a circle.

"My dear," he looked down upon the new bride, "as you know from your Bible study, Ephesians Chapter 5: Verses 22 through 24 outlines a wife's designated position of submission in marriage." He cleared his throat. "Yes, this New Testament verse prescribes to us: Wives, submit yourselves unto your own husbands, as unto the Lord. The husband is the head of the wife, as Christ is the head of the Church, and He is the savior of the body. Therefore, as the Church is subject unto Christ, so *let* the wives *be* to their own husbands in everything."

The man wiped beads of perspiration from his glistening forehead, although it was a cool spring evening.

"Gertie," he continued, "do you understand what this means?"

"I think so."

"It means," he ignored her response, "that you may discuss any conflicts that you have with Peter, but in the end, you must do as he decides. Should a wife fail her husband, the Lord instructs the husband to correct her as appropriate. Now, do you understand?"

Gertie had understood him the first time. She was aware her father ruled the household and her mother, as the Lord prescribed. Thus, she nodded her comprehension of the Preacher's instructions.

"Excellent. And you Peter, do you understand your obligation to Gertie?"

"I do, sir."

Again, the Preacher ignored the response. "It is written that the husband's duty is to ensure that his wife is obedient to himself and thus to God. In doing so, he presents his love for his wife. For there can be no greater love than God's love for his chosen people. The chosen people pledged love and obedience to God and God rebuked them when they failed in their commitment. Therefore, as a wife has pledged love and obedience to her husband."

Peter nodded.

Undaunted, the Preacher continued, "Peter, it is also written that you must love your wife as you love your God. This means you must put her wellbeing before all others—before your own. If after toiling all day, you can only put one meal on the table, that meal shall be hers. In this way, you two," he paused to radiate a smile down upon them, "are united. Caring for each other, as the Lord cares for you. You two are now joined as one. Bow your heads." Placing his hands on their heads, he completed the blessing.

"Amen," the three said in unison.

During the lecture, the wedding party had prepared their buggy for departure. When the couple exited the church, the rows of cheering family and friends showered them with rice and confetti. Peter escorted Gertie to the waiting buggy. Waving goodbye and grinning from ear to ear, Gertie watched her mother and father fade away.

She was alone with her new husband. She had never been alone with a man before. Silence and darkness surrounded them. Gertie pulled her shawl tightly around her shoulders and pressed her body towards Peter's warmth.

"As you know," he swallowed before saying her Christian name for the first time, "Gertie, I have already sold my house. We will stay in the boarding house where I have been living until the end of the week."

"Yes... Peter."

Gertie watched the street lanterns of Cincinnati spread to the horizon as the buggy descended the hill on the northwest side of town. Ohio had been her home since she turned eleven years old. She could remember no trepidation when her family had emigrated from Germany to America in 1840. They had been poor, starving tenant farmers in economically depressed Germany. The past eight years had been the happiest of her life as the farm that her father actually owned had thrived. Now, she was not only having to adjust to married life, she was going to have to adjust to living in the Oregon Territory. The German immigrants followed the Old World customs and Mr. Berg was a second son and not eligible to inherit the family farm. He was employed at a dry goods store, but had sold his property in preparation to take the Oregon Trail west before his first wife had died. They had intended to seek out land for themselves. In marrying him, Gertie was accepting this fate. And this, as much as the looming wedding night, was giving her chills.

Peter guided the buggy along the waterfront road. The clattering iron wheels on the cobblestones of the wharf-front road alerted Gertie to the end of their trip. She examined the steamboats docked along the Ohio River, wondering which one would take her away from everything she knew and loved. Peter pulled back on the reins and halted the horse in front of the Queen Anne boarding house. A porter collected her valise and followed as Peter led his bride to her matrimonial chamber. Gertie was actually glad he was not taking her to the house where he had lived with his other wife—the house where she and their baby had died.

At the threshold of their room, he scooped her up in his powerful arms and carried her inside. Gertie giggled as he gently returned her feet to the floor. With a finger, he tilted her face upward and kissed her. This time, he took his time. This time, he held her close and savored her tender lips.

Yes, marriage is going to be very nice.

Gertie closed her eyes and pressed her body into his; her spine tingled.

The porter cleared his throat. "Will there be anything else, sir?" He put her valise on the bed and lit several candles

"No," Peter said. After waiting for the porter to depart, he continued, "I'll be in the washroom down the hall." He needlessly pointed. "There is a chamber pot there," he nodded toward the wooden box in the corner. "And everything else you might need." He turned away. "I'll be back in a few minutes."

When he closed the door, Gertie examined the ten by ten foot room. She unbuttoned the gown she had borrowed from her mother, and hung it in the wardrobe. She stripped off her blouse and bodice. She rolled down her stockings and used the chamber pot. Finally, she untied the ribbons which held her chemise closed and examined her lanky, nude body in the mirror. She wondered what Peter would think of her.

What had his first wife looked like? Was she pretty? Gertie wondered

After this night she would be a real woman. Soon she would achieve the final step in a woman's maturity and become a mother.

Gertie unpacked her bag and poured water from the pitcher into the basin. She added lavender scent, a gift from her sister, to the water. After rinsing her body, she pulled on her nightdress. Instead of donning her sleeping bonnet, she brushed out the braids in her straw-colored hair. Blowing out all but one of the candles, she slid under the bed cover. She lay on her back and waited.

When Peter returned, he quietly crept into the room as though avoiding disturbing her. Wearing his nightshirt, he carried his clothing in a bundle. She silently watched as he placed his clothes atop hers. Embarrassingly, she had forgotten to conceal her chemise and underskirt. Now, his gray woolen trousers and white cotton shirt were intermingled with the lace of her undergarments. However, he took no notice.

Peter extinguished the last candle. Illuminated by the slivers of light around the curtain, Gertie watched her husband pull off his nightshirt. The newlyweds lay side by side under the bed cover, panting with anticipation—excitement. She expected that he knew what to do next.

"Are you asleep?" he whispered.

"No," she whispered back.

He rolled to his side and placed his hand on her abdomen. Touching her in the manner only a husband could touch his wife. Her flesh tingled.

Yes, this is it!

In the darkness, Gertie could hear the sounds of people talking in the distance. She worried that they might know what was happening in the small room.

He nuzzled against her shoulder. His beard both tickled and scratched her neck. She wondered what she should be doing with her hands. He kissed her and she placed a hand on the back of his neck. She did not want him to stop.

Oh, my God!

A burst of thudding of hoof beats came from the street below as a horse galloped by. She thought of the people outside, going about their evening activities, hopefully unaware of what was transpiring a few feet away.

Peter broke their kiss and nuzzled his forehead against the side of her head. His hand inched up her torso.

She gasped.

"Are you all right?" he whispered.

"Yes, I'm sorry."

"No need to be. I don't mean to rush you."

She swallowed the lump in her throat and pulled his lips back to hers. She could smell the smoke from the candle and the scent of the soap used to wash the bedsheets. This was her wedding night and she wanted to remember every detail.

CHAPTER TWO

April 16, 1848
Fort Union, Northwest Wilderness

The heavy wooden door swung open, allowing the north wind to wreak its cold vengeance upon the log cabin's interior. Edgar Millar had found the long January nights along the Canadian border to be unbearable. It had been a cold which could leave you frozen and dead, lost until the spring thaw and wild animals found your remains. Although warmer temperatures had accompanied the arrival of spring, the strong wind blowing down from the ice capped Rocky Mountains still chilled him to the bone.

The intruder stood, holding the door open. Edgar squinted as the bright sunlight silhouetted the figure of a man. Edgar opened his mouth to tell the man to *close the darn door*, but the stranger spoke first.

"Bart's dead."

Edgar sucked in a breath. While the cold air stung his nostrils, his sinuses were grateful for the brief reprieve from the stench of the drying buffalo hides.

"What? Dead?"

"Aye, he drowned." Edgar recognized the voice of Alistair McKinsey, one of the few old-time mountain men still fur trapping.

"Bart drowned? How?"

"He tried to walk across the Yellowstone. The ice gave way."

During the long winter, both the Yellowstone and Missouri Rivers had frozen over, allowing men to walk over them. However, with the early spring the ice covering had thinned and would no longer support the weight of a full grown man.

"What made him do that?" Edgar asked. Bart was a very experienced mountain man not prone to foolish risks.

"Because he was a dern fool." McKinsey stepped across the threshold and closed the door. "He shot an elk on the other side, and thought he could walk on water."

Bart Adams had hired Edgar Millar down south, in Independence, Missouri. "Watch my back, boy. Make sure no one stabs me in my sleep," the burly old mountain man had said.

Edgar had little idea what the man would require of him, but he had been down on his luck and in bad need of a job. Edgar learned later that Adams had just sold his collection of hides and furs. The sale had garnered Bart hundreds of dollars in gold coins which filled a canvas money belt the older man stashed inside his shirt. Adams bartered with several merchants for supplies and trade goods. With their heavy load, the two men had boarded the steamboat bound up the Missouri River to Fort Union.

Located at the junction of the Yellowstone and Missouri Rivers, Fort Union was the northern most inhabited town in the territories now owned by the United States. With the Louisiana Purchase in 1803, the land drained by the Mississippi and Missouri Rivers had become part of the young North American nation. Upon their arrival in Fort Union, Edgar learned he had been hired to operate the trading post owned by Mr. Adams.

Millar shook the memories from his mind and returned his attention to McKinsey as he continued, "He ain't been all together since Wyalla died," McKinsey said of Bart's state of mind.

Wyalla, Bart's Indian wife, had caught the fever and died in February. Edgar had observed the steady waning of Bart attention on the business of the trading post, but his lack of sensibility had begun months before Wyalla had died. "The fur trade is dead," he had said to Edgar in January. "I'm gonna sell out. I'm taking Wyalla south to Texas. Gonna buy a ranch and grow old. You'll be wise to do the same, but tell no one else."

John Jacob Astor had founded Fort Union back in 1828, at the height of the fur trade business. Fort Union was a civilian establishment fashioned after a military bastion. In the old days, its cannon protected the American Fur Company headquarters from Indian attack. Now, it was a sanctuary settlement. It was a place where English, French, Americans, and Indians of various tribes could come and go freely despite the changing political winds of their respective homelands. Without regard as to who may be at war with whom, the settlement was currently at peace.

Fort Union had grown from its original 300 square-foot encampment to a town of more than a hundred citizens. These included carpenters, blacksmiths, Jesuit priests, and saloon girls. Unfortunately, civilized fashions had changed and the demand for beaver and other furs had fallen. In 1842 Astor sold the trading post to Bart Adams. Not only a hunter and tracker but also skilled at bargaining, Bart had been able to maintain a good living trading food and supplies for deer and buffalo hides. He had haggled and bargained with the Indians and the few mountain men who remained. As time went by, Bart had seen the end of their business was near. He had wisely decided to quit, but just not soon enough.

"Where is he now? His body?"

"Uh, I expect it's half way to Independence by now." McKinsey smirked. He made a motion with his hands indicating that Bart's body was flowing with the river, under the ice.

Edgar spotted the rifle slung across McKinsey's back.

"Is that Bart's Hawken?" Frowning, Edgar extended his hand and waited. The Hawken rifle was valuable. Most mountain men carried a nearly four-foot long Kentucky style rifle. While known for their accuracy, the long rifles were heavy and difficult to reload. Adams owned a newer Plains style rifle produced by the Hawken brothers. This rifle was distinctive in that it was 18 inches shorter.

Adams had no next of kin, thus, Edgar reasoned what Bart had owned was now his to inherit. Edgar had worked for Bart for the past year and they had become trusted friends. He had used his education to work as Bart's accountant in addition to clerking in the trading post. He had augmented his income with some hunting of his own.

McKinsey licked his lips and adjusted the strap weighing on his shoulder. "Aye, it is." He made no move to hand it over.

"I'm much obliged to you for bringing it to me." Edgar stared into the man's dark eyes. "We were partners, Bart and me. Signed the papers and all," Edgar lied. However, he imagined that if Bart had ever given the matter a moment's thought, he would have willed all of his property to Edgar.

"Aye," McKinsey swallowed, "that's what I done. I brung it to ye." He passed the rifle to Edgar.

Examining the weapon, Edgar wondered how it was that Bart Adams had fallen through the ice while his rifle remained high and dry. He thought of what other valuables Bart might have been carrying. Thinking of nothing specific, he did not press the issue with McKinsey further.

"Thank you."

"So, what will ye be doing now, with all this?" McKinsey swept his arm across the cabin, gesturing to the piles of hides and the stacks of trade goods. Edgar realized the true purpose of the man's visit. He had probably murdered Bart, or at least hastened his death, with the intention of taking possession of the trading post.

"I reckon, it's all mine now." Edgar knew he would be getting rid of as much as he could and taking the hides south on the first steamboat once the ice broke. He would not be coming back, but he was not going to tell Alistair McKinsey that tidbit of information. "I expect that I will be needing to acquire a partner though." To buy time, Edgar needed to give McKinsey a reason not to murder him as well.

Alistair's face brightened. "My brother might be interested. He's not much for the hunting anymore."

"Hmm, yes, Corbin would be a fine man to take on. Does he have the cash to buy in?"

Edgar reasoned that McKinsey had murdered Bart. The man wanted the trading post for himself, but had not anticipated Edgar's resistance. With the invitation to become partners, Edgar was forestalling a confrontation with the brothers. They would eventually drive him out or murder him, but they would bide their time. This would allow Edgar to make his departure with Bart Adams' hidden stash of money.

* * *

Cincinnati, Ohio

The morning following her wedding, Gertie Berg pretended not to watch her husband, but she did. She watched as he swung his legs to the floor and stood up from the bed. Her younger sister had been the only person she had ever seen naked before she saw Peter's bare butt. His was entirely different from Ida's round posterior. Despite Peter's other round features, his bottom looked like a flat deflated balloon.

Peter picked up his shirt and put it on. Gertie caught a glimpse of his manhood—gone was its rigidity. It was small and flaccid; she wondered how he managed this tool.

He pulled on his trousers, lifted the suspenders to his shoulders, and stuffed his feet into his boots. He turned to look at her and she was caught staring.

"Wait here," he said, ignoring that she had been watching him. "I'll get you some breakfast."

Gertie reasoned is was normal for husband and wife to look at each other. She wondered when he would ask to see her in the bare.

She opened her mouth, but no sound came out. She nodded.

As soon as he left, she hastened to use the chamber pot. She quickly dressed in the light gray day-frock which she packed in her valise. She rolled on her stockings and was tying the garters behind her knees when he opened the door. He had not knocked.

Peter placed the breakfast tray on the washstand. He did not avert his eyes despite having discovered her with her legs scandalously exposed. She made no move to cover herself until she finished with the placement of her stockings.

"Here," he said, "I intended for you to have breakfast in bed this morning."

"Oh, that is very thoughtful of you. And I shall." As she was shoeless, she reclined on the bed. He placed the tray of scrambled eggs, bacon, and fried potato cake beside her. "Thank you, very much... Peter."

She watched his eyes trace along her exposed calves to her feet. For some inexplicable reason, she wiggled her toes.

"I'm off to work this morning," he said. "Feel free to come by the store so I can introduce you to my friends."

"Yes, I will. However, first I must return to Papa's farm. I need to begin packing for the trip to Oregon."

"Yes, about that... Gertie, you must remember that we can take very little with us. Only what is essential."

"Won't we have one of those big wagons?"

"Indeed, but it will be filled with our provisions for the trip. It is a four-month trek and the wagon will be filled with food and supplies. There's simply no room for a collection of niceties."

"Yes, of course, I understand."

After collecting Mr. Berg's buggy and horse from the livery stable, Gertie drove the three miles northwest to her family farm. Her father and brother were working in the fields, but her mother greeted her warmly. Her sister Ida was full of smiles and giggles, and pulled her aside at the first opportunity.

"How was it? Really?" Ida whispered, anticipating her own wedding night.

Gertie did her best to look like a full-grown woman of the world, as though the experience had changed her—matured her. With casual distraction, she answered, "Oh, it was pleasant enough. Don't let the old women scare you. It doesn't really hurt enough to bother mentioning." Gertie searched for the words to explain that Peter had repeated the lovemaking act twice more during the night. "It gets better with each time you repeat it." Embarrassed, she turned her eyes away.

Gertie selected the three largest trunks in the attic. She and Ida began to fill them with everything she owned. At lunchtime, her mother came to call them to dinner.

"I didn't imagine that you could take so much all the way to Oregon? Are you having that shipped?" she asked.

"Shipped?"

"Yes, on a schooner around South America to Oregon?"

"Is such a thing possible?"

"I don't know about these things, but I do know there are ships which make the voyage."

"Hmm, well, I expect we will take this with us. Mr. Berg is securing us a big wagon." Her mother opened her mouth as though to say something, but closed it.

"No one can expect us to travel so far with only the clothes on our backs. Mr. Berg will see my way of thinking, I'm sure."

Again, her mother appeared to have some words on the tip of her tongue, but she held them.

After lunch, they loaded the trunks onto the buggy and Gertie returned to the boarding house. Two men helped her carry them up the stairs and stack them in the corner of their small room. By the time this was completed, it was late in the afternoon and she was tired; she had not gotten much sleep the night before.

Gertie lay down on the bed and closed her eyes. She dreamed of green fields dotted with yellow flowers. She imagined this to be the Oregon Territory.

"What is this, Mrs. Berg?"

For a moment Gertie did not recognize Peter's voice or that the voice was talking to her. She rolled onto her side and rubbed the sleep from her eyes. She opened them to the blurry vision of her new husband.

"I'm sorry, Mr. Berg, I didn't get much sleep last night." She responded with the same formality of his speech.

"You said that you would come to the shop. I told my friends that you would be there."

"I, uh, well, it took more time than I imagined to pack my things." Gertie gestured to the stacked trunks in the corner.

"Mrs. Berg—" Peter paused to take a deep breath and scoff before continuing in a softer tone. "Gertie, we discussed these matters this morning. You agreed to visit the shop and to limit your baggage to a single trunk."

"Yes, I know, but—"

"If you have need to change the plan, you are required to discuss it with me first. We are married and now make the decisions together."

"Yes, I am sorry, but I don't see how you can expect me to move to the other side of the world with just one trunk for my clothes and things."

"As we discussed this morning," Peter was having difficulty keeping his tone under control, "there simply isn't room. Take only those things you *must* have. You can make new clothes when we get there."

"Can we not have them shipped?" Gertie borrowed the term from her mother.

"*No*, that is not possible. Do you have any idea how *much* that would cost?"

Gertie slowly shook her head; his tone implied it would cost a great deal of money.

"Come here," Peter commanded. He pulled the chair from the washstand and sat in it. He patted his thigh.

"Oh, no, Mr. Berg, you can't mean to—" He had assumed the posture her father used to punish her.

"I most certainly do."

"But—" she took a breath.

"I won't be harsh—if you submit *now*." He retrieved her hairbrush from the table.

She realized that she had reached the end of her rope. If she persisted, he would overpower her and the sounds of the tussle would certainly draw the notice of everyone in the boarding house. To avoid this humiliation, she surrendered.

Gertie rose from the bed and took the three steps to her husband's side. She bent over his lap. Peter lifted the hairbrush and she closed her eyes.

Gertie offered no resistance in an effort to hurry him along. Embarrassed as she was, she would be mortified if those in the hallway were to become aware of what was occurring.

"Now, tell me what you are going to do to correct your transgressions?"

"My dear husband, tomorrow I will return two of the trunks to my father's house and I will bring you a luncheon at the store."

"Excellent, but as you select those items to keep in the one trunk, remember to leave room for my belongings as well."

Gertie grunted her displeasure with this new restriction, but said, "Yes." Thinking it might be a good idea to appease him at this moment, she added, "I'm sorry, sir."

Peter directed her to sit on his lap and hugged her. He kissed her tenderly. Thus far, kissing was her favorite aspect of being married.

"Mrs. Brunt has supper on the table. Let's go down and eat. I'll introduce you to our fellow boarders," he said, when their lips parted.

Gertie's face flushed with embarrassment, thinking they might know what had transpired, but she took Peter's hand and followed him out the door.

CHAPTER THREE

May 7, 1848
Independence, Missouri

Heralded by the blaring sound of the steam whistle, Gertie and Peter disembarked from the steamboat for the last time.

"Must they always make that hideous noise," Gertie remarked.

Peter chuckled. "It's to dump off the excess steam in the boilers."

Gertie grunted, expressing her dissatisfaction with his answer and with the effort to lift her side of their trunk. She and Peter had carried this trunk for several miles in the past three weeks. She had become ever so grateful he had insisted on taking only *one* trunk on their voyage. Peter hoisted the second handle and they walked down the gangplank to the dock.

In the preceding three weeks, Mr. and Mrs. Berg had ridden a steamboat down the Ohio River from Cincinnati to Paducah, Kentucky, where they boarded a boat to St. Louis. The pace of the steamboat traveling upriver on the Missouri was much slower than traveling downriver on the Ohio. After a frustrating delay, they completed this final watery leg of the trip to Oregon aboard a cramped and crowded boat from St. Louis to Independence, Missouri.

Along the way, Gertie had read pamphlets describing their pending trip west and learned a great deal about wagon trains and the Oregon Territory. Contrasting the cold Ohio winters, the pamphlets spoke of the wonderful climate, rich soil, and the wealth of lumber promised in the Willamette Valley. Five years earlier settlers had begun using the unofficial pathway labeled the Oregon Trail. The report and maps created by John C Fremont, the Great Pathfinder, was the bible for these travelers. In 1841, Congress had hired him to explore the west in preparation for future settling. Gertie had found reading the detailed explorations taxing and had quickly skimmed the pages.

As a result of the recent agreement with Great Britain, Americans were being granted 320 acres of land just for migrating to Oregon. Thousands of people, like herself and Peter, had insufficient funds to buy land and no hope of inheriting it. Thus, this lure of free, fertile farmland was irresistible. With this westward rush, the Trail had become much more of a highway with thousands of wagons making the trip each year.

The majority of these travelers gathered their belongings into a wagon and began the long overland trek from their homes. A smaller number of the more well-to-do traveled the first half of the journey along the river, as she and Peter had done. While a faster and easier trip, it forced them to travel light and to purchase their final supplies upon reaching Independence.

Gertie knew Independence was the farthest west the steamboat traveled. From this point, the Missouri River turned almost due north. Independence, on the south side of the river was the westernmost location where travelers could jump-off, as it was called. The wagon trains had to depart from the south side of the river because the Missouri was too deep for the heavy cumbersome wagons to cross. From this point, they would work their way 200 miles northward to the Platte River and then follow it for a thousand miles west. It was a long dangerous journey that many started but not all had survived.

While others found this an exciting adventure, Gertie longed for the comfort of her soft bed in her father's house. However, she was a married woman now. For better or for worse, she and Peter were united on this trek. She suppressed all hint of complaint from her voice. Peter's repeated disciplinary reactions had finally curbed her opinionated tongue.

"Pardon my intrusion." Peter waved a passerby to a stop. "Kind sir, do you happen to know where can we find Major Jamison and his wagon train?"

"All the trains are assembling over there," the man pointed down a long road to the south. Gertie saw nothing but an open grass field extending to the far hillside. "Ask anyone there for additional directions." The stranger tipped his hat to Mrs. Berg.

Thinking of herself to be more of a pack mule than a wife, she held her valise in her left hand and picked up the trunk handle in her right hand. Peter held the opposite side and his valise. The pair followed a dozen other emigrants along the dusty road. They walked for more than a mile before topping a hill. Gertie's arms ached. Sweat ran down her back and between her breasts when they stopped to rest. From the hillcrest, she studied the vast prairie filled with wagons and encampments as far as the eye could see.

"There must be hundreds of them," Gertie exclaimed. She had not imagined the Oregon Trail would be such a huge enterprise.

They walked along the row of white tents displaying the names of the various wagon train leaders. When they found the sign identifying their train they left their belongings outside and entered the tent.

"Major Jamison, I presume. I am Mr. Peter Berg and this is my wife Gertie." She nodded when Peter gestured toward her.

"Pleasure to meet you, sir, ma'am." He touched the brim of his hat and nodded in her direction. "But I am not Major Jamison."

"Oh, I sent word of our arrival and intention to join the Major's wagon train for Oregon."

"Indeed, sir, I'm not arguing the point. I am Daniel Woodstock, the Major's assistant on this train. I'll check you in." The man leafed through a stack of papers. "Ah, here you are. Yes, you will be in site 22-C. That's here," he pointed to a grid drawn on a chalkboard. "We are here, and row C is the third one back, and here is site twenty-two." With an air of finality, he tapped on a spot on the chalk outline. "That will be fifty dollars, in advance—gold."

Peter stepped aside and turned his back while fumbling through the pouch on his belt. He handed the gold coins to Mr. Woodstock. The man wrote a receipt and passed it to Peter.

"Keep yer livestock inside your assigned site."

"Sir, we don't yet have a wagon and oxen. Where can I acquire them?"

Mr. Woodstock's eyebrow shot up and he studied Peter. "The money is not refundable." His eyes narrowed. "I suggest you get a rig very quickly. The carpenter is back in town, and there is a stock dealer as well, but it has all been picked over by now."

"Thank you, I shall do just that."

The two retrieved their belongings and began counting the campsites as they trudged along the rows of prairie schooners. Finding 22-C, they dropped their burdens with a sigh of relief.

"You wait here. I'll go fetch a wagon and oxen."

Peter left Gertie sitting atop their trunk. She turned to watch two children, a boy about five and his older sister, playing in the shade of the wagon parked in site 22-D. The sites were each about a hundred feet square to allow a grazing area for the livestock. The covered wagon in 22-D was positioned close to their shared boundary with their four oxen tethered to stakes in the ground on the opposite side. A horse grazed among the huge beasts which were taller at their shoulders than Gertie. While the wagon was large, it was smaller than the Conestoga wagons used to haul freight in Ohio and the Eastern States. Gertie knew from the guidebook that the soil of the western prairie was too soft to support the heavier wagons. Additionally, there were no bridges across the rivers and their muddy bottoms would not support the wheels. This wagon was about four feet wide, ten feet in length, and three feet deep. The wagon box, as the passenger seat was known, was attached to the front. From the ground to the top of the white, canvas bonnet was ten feet. The front and rear ends of the bonnet were cantilevered outward to shade the ends of the wagon.

When the wind slacked, Gertie heard a distinctive sound. She strained to hear better and smiled while she listened to the rhythmic pattern of grunts and moans of lovemaking. The couple was doubtlessly unaware they now had neighbors. Being with so many people, so close together, she suspected privacy would be minimal.

The sounds ended and moments later the woman climbed down from the rear of the wagon. Not realizing Gertie was present, she adjusted her garments and bent over the pot which was suspended above the cooking fire.

Gertie was uncertain whether to make her presence known, or not, but the issue was put to rest when the woman's husband jumped down.

"Why, hello, madam, do pardon my wife's inattention. We were not aware that we had a new neighbor." The man removed his hat and bowed. Gertie stood and acknowledged his politeness with a brief curtsey. She had never seen a Mormon before. However, she had heard many tales of their eccentric life. While this man's distinctive dress and sculptured beard were instantly recognizable, he did not appear to be either magical or blasphemous.

Where are his other wives?

After initially founding Kirtland, Ohio, the Mormons had left to seek religious freedom further west—before Gertie had emigrated from Germany. They had founded Independence, Missouri, but had been driven out as the Gentile population increased. In 1848, the majority of the settlers in the land between the Missouri River and the Pacific coast were Mormons. They were the ones who opened up the West.

"I am Abram Smoot, this is my wife, Martha, and these are our two children, Elijah and Ruth." He gestured to the two children who remained distracted with their toys.

"I'm pleased to meet you. I'm Gertie and that," she pointed to the shrinking figure walking away, "is my husband Peter Berg."

"Where is he going?" Abram asked.

"He is off to purchase a rig for us. We arrived on the steamboat only a few hours ago."

"Does he need any assistance? Does he know which dealers are liars and thieves?"

Gertie shrugged. "He might appreciate some assistance. As we just arrived, I doubt he knows one dealer from another."

"Well, let me see what I can do." Abram untied his horse and mounted it bareback. "Martha, make our new friend at home." He tapped his heels into the animal's flanks. With the animal at a trot, he set off to catch up with Peter.

Instantly, Gertie regretted the exchange. She had no idea what Peter's disposition toward Mormons was, and she considered he might not appreciate Abram's assistance. Peter might not be interested in hearing her explanation of how she had not really sent Abram to help.

Martha's face flushed as she approached. Gertie did her best to keep her expression neutral, to hide what she knew of the woman's activity.

"I am preparing some beans for a ham stew." She looked around at the meager collection of Gertie's possessions. "Do you have anything to eat? Please, won't you and your husband join us for supper?"

"Thank you very much for your kind offer. However, I must confer with my husband before accepting your invitation."

Martha presented a knowing smile as she demonstrated that she understood a wife's boundary. "Yes, of course, but know that the offer stands. Please, come sit in the shade. We can watch your things from here." She beckoned Gertie to join her and the children on the tarpaulin beside their wagon.

"Thank you." Gertie was pleased to join her and the two women sat with the children beside the wagon. The prairie breeze in the shade cooled her and Gertie pulled her shawl snug around her shoulders. "Are you going to Oregon?" Gertie had heard of a Mormon settlement in Oregon.

"No, we are heading for the New Kingdom beside the Great Salt Lake. Now that the war with Mexico is over, this land is open to American settlers."

"I see, but aren't these wagon trains for the Oregon Trail?"

Gertie watched the far hillside as Abram met with Peter. The two men talked and looked back toward the encampment. Abram dismounted and walked beside Peter, leading his horse. The two men disappeared over the hill. From what little she could see, Peter did not appear to be vexed.

"You are correct," Martha answered, "but the Mormon Trail and the Oregon Trail are the same until they split at Fort Bridger—on the other side of South Pass. Your wagon train and ours will be fairly close together for a long time. We will certainly see each other along the way."

"South Pass?"

"Yes, it is the pathway through the mountains. Oregon Territory is on the western side; however the land you seek is still a thousand mile further west."

Gertie sighed, trying to imagine the vast distance and the effort that lay before them.

Seeing her frown, Martha patted Gertie's hand. "Don't fret, my dear, a thousand or more people have made the journey. You will make it too."

The accounts of the trek Gertie had read were written by those who had turned back. Lacking sufficient supplies, or experiencing illness, or for any number reasons—these people had quit the journey and returned home. All of these had turned back before reaching Fort John. This was the halfway point, and there was no reason to turn back after passing this point. Thus, there were no accounts published by those who had successfully completed the trip.

Undoubtedly Martha is right. Most all travelers complete the journey safely.

Gertie swallowed the lump in her throat and forced a smile to her face as she pushed the dread from her mind. "Who are all those other people?" Gertie waved her arm across the southern horizon.

Martha followed her gaze. While the four trains were organized in the neat square plots, the remainder of the valley was a disorganized jumble of campsites. Several prairie schooners were weaving through the disorganization, heading westward.

"Now that the trail is so well marked, most people choose to travel on their own instead of with the organized wagon trains," Martha replied. "While this saves money, it requires each family to be completely self-sufficient. Our wagonmasters, Major Jamison for you and Mr. Hatch for me, provide such things as spare wagon wheels and oxen should we have a mishap. Also, they have cows for fresh milk. The wranglers keep track of our livestock and the scouts hunt for fresh meat. All this means that we can spend more time traveling and less time providing for ourselves. Thus, we make the trip in a shorter span of time than they do." Martha jutted her chin toward the throng of small campsites.

Gertie realized the wisdom in Peter's decision to spend fifty dollars on Major Jamison's expertise. She would not want to be in the vast wilderness on her own.

"Not needing to pack such extras," Martha continued, "we can pack more of our personal possessions." She cast an eye toward Gertie's meager collection of belongings.

"We came by steamboat," she needlessly responded. Gertie had no idea how much of their money Peter had spent, but she would make-do with whatever he provided. She would make no complaints, not even to another woman.

"Don't worry, dearie, we'll help you out. Is your husband skilled with managing oxen?" Martha asked. "I only ask because so many of the families in the wagon trains are from cities and have no such skills. Oxen are rather difficult to control."

"I don't really know. We've only been married a short while." Gertie did not say exactly how short of a time. "However, his family owned a farm outside of Cincinnati, Ohio, and he has never expressed any doubts to me."

Three hours later, as dusk enveloped them, Peter and Abram returned riding atop a wagon drawn by two huge oxen. Abram's horse was tethered behind the wagon. Gertie noticed Peter was all smiles, but she held her tongue until she got a better sense of his mood.

The two men parked the wagon in 22-C, but near Abram's wagon. Peter had purchased a wagon which was two-thirds the length of the Smoot's wagon. However, it was pulled by only one yoke of oxen—two oxen per yoke. The Smoot wagon carried the supplies for the family of four and required two yoke of oxen. While he had not discussed the matter with her, Gertie saw the correctness of Peter's selection. They would have a much easier time managing the smaller wagon.

The two men unhitched the oxen and tethered them where they could eat the grass. Peter followed Abram to join Gertie and Martha. Abram introduced Peter to Martha.

Peter turned to Gertie. "See, Gertie, we are meeting good fortune. We have already made new friends. Mr. Smoot is a great negotiator and we struck a fine deal." He beamed. "No one knew where new wagons could be found, but Mr. Smoot knew the merchants, and we found this one. It had been owned by a couple struck by illness and decided to return home."

Gertie was unsettled with this ill omen, but held her tongue.

"The wagon is filled with most of what we need. Tomorrow we will begin purchasing our remaining provisions. Tonight, we sleep in our new home." He gestured to the covered wagon as though it was a castle.

"You are joining us for supper, are you not?" Martha injected, before Gertie could respond.

Peter glanced at Gertie and she nodded ever so slightly. "Thank you, madam; we will be delighted to accept your hospitality," Peter responded.

They ate the simple meal while sitting on the tarp in the shade of the wagon. After eating, the newlyweds bid goodbye to their new friends and returned to their own camp. They removed the contents of the wagon and sorted their new belongings on the ground. They had bolts of canvas for tents, hundreds of feet of rope, various wooden and iron stakes, tools, and cooking utensils—Dutch oven, frying pan, coffee pot, tin plates and cups, and knives, forks and spoons.

Peter had not purchased anything for their bed, but Gertie said nothing. She was delighted to have some privacy. During the week on the steamboat from St. Louis, all of the passengers lived together in the communal salon. There had been no privacy. They had slept in their clothes. As meager as it was, this wagon was the first thing which they owned together. Gertie spread out some of the canvas on the floor of the wagon to create a sleeping palette. The interior of the wagon was barely large enough for them to sleep side-by-side. She changed into her nightdress and made love with her husband in their new home. Gertie was definitely enjoying matrimony.

"I spent the last of our paper money," Peter whispered as he held her close. Without further explanation, Gertie understood the significance of his statement.

There were no banks in the wilderness west of Independence and only gold and silver coins would be accepted as money. Peter had deliberately divested himself of the paper money that would soon be worthless. "Tomorrow we will begin buying the needed supplies—flour, yeast, bacon. I want you to select bolts of cloth that you can use to make us new clothes once we reach our new land. I'm sure these clothes will be worn out by then."

Gertie nodded and began creating a mental list of the things she would need to sew their new items of clothing. She enjoyed sewing and was quite good at it. Her thoughts put a smile on her face.

CHAPTER FOUR

May 15, 1848
Independence, Missouri

Peter and Gertie stocked their rig for the four-month journey to Oregon. Their food staple would be wild game meat, but they purchased a hundred and fifty pounds of bacon for those days when fresh meat was unavailable. The primary accompaniment would be bread and thus they purchased seven 20-pound bags of flour. These were double wrapped and stored in wooden barrels. For corn bread and griddle cakes they purchased six 20-pound bags of corn meal. Completing their food supply was ten pounds of coffee, fifteen pounds of molasses, five pounds of honey, ten pounds of salt, and assorted dried fruits. Additionally, as suggested by Major Jamison, they bought supplies to trade with the Indians—beads, tobacco, blankets, cheap clothing, butcher knives, and fishhooks. The interior of the wagon was filled; the only open space was the wagon box attached to the front. This is where Gertie imagined she would ride for most of the trip while Peter walked alongside the oxen, directing them. While many of the emigrants would sleep in tents alongside their rigs, Gertie used their spare canvas to prepare a bed, and placed this over the top of their goods. Wary of the creatures to be found in the wilderness, she was afraid of sleeping on the ground and desired additional privacy.

Thus equipped, Peter and Gertie took their place as the twenty-second wagon among the fifty wagon long line of travelers seeking a new life. The four wagon trains, staged in Independence, departed at first light. Peter snapped the long birch whip on the backs of the oxen and they took the first step of their two thousand mile journey. In the beginning, the four trains ran in parallel, a hundred feet apart with their extra livestock grazing along between the long rows of wagons. Wranglers rode ahead and cleared a path through the other more disorganized travelers. Most of these were men venturing out on the Oregon Trail alone. They had banded together in groups of three or four wagons as they pulled away earlier than the rest. These first smaller groups had hoped to make better time ahead of the long lines of wagons that followed. The chaos of leaving had created a confused mass of cows, horses, and men afoot moving among the wagons.

As explained by Major Jamison, their departure date had been carefully selected. The trip across the vast plains of the Indian Territory had to be completed before the first autumn snows in the western mountains. The trail through the mountains was impassable in the snow. However, they could not leave Independence until after the spring grass had grown. If they departed too soon, the oxen and other livestock would starve without the spring growth for grazing. Added to the departure calculation was the need to wait for the spring floods to pass. They would cross many rivers, and these crossings would be too dangerous with the rivers swollen by the spring rains. The very surge of waters which had created the navigable channel for their trip up the Missouri River now hampered their departure.

The oxen plodded along at something close to the walking pace of a man. Gertie knew horses could draw the wagon faster, but they wouldn't have the stamina to pull the wagon day after day for two thousand miles.

Hours of slow wagon travel later, they prepared to make their first river crossing. River crossings were the most dangerous aspect of the trip. They would have to make scores of crossings before they reached Oregon. Most of these would have to be completed with little or no assistance. However, for this first one, teams of men on horseback were ready to help the novice travelers cross the Blue River.

Peter paid a dime to each of three riders. They tied ropes to the front and back of the wagon, and a third line on the ox yoke. The men rode their horses upstream of the wagon to steady it against the current.

"No matter what," one of the men cautioned Peter, "don't stop. If you stop, then you will sink into the mud. The wagon will tip over and you will be in a real mess."

Terrified, Gertie held on for dear life as they rolled into the swirling, brown water. The wagon was constructed much like a small flatbed boat and now Gertie understood this wisdom. There were moments when the wagon floated completely free, but their assistants kept it from drifting with the current. Some of the families attempted to cross without the assistance of the horsemen. Two of these did tip over, and had to be towed to shore and righted. Gertie had no idea how much damage to their belongings occurred. The main body of the wagon train did not wait for these two unfortunate families. Major Jamison had specified the number of miles they had to achieve before camping. Somehow, those left behind would just have to catch up, or turn back.

From the pamphlets she had scanned, Gertie knew their general route. They would follow the Kaw River west until they found a safe crossing point. Once across the river, they would turn northwest. The next major river crossing was the South Platte River, a hundred miles to the northwest. The rivers were lined with thick groves of cottonwood trees, otherwise the prairie was an unbroken expanse of grass.

At dusk they had completed ten miles. The four wagon trains were camped for the night at half-mile intervals. Gertie could see the campfire of her friend, Martha, in the camp behind theirs, but she was too tired and too busy cooking to walk over for a visit.

"Evening, ma'am." Major Jamison and Mr. Woodstock tipped their hats; Gertie smiled and nodded.

"Good evening, Major," Peter replied.

"How is your rig? Did everything work properly today? Any breakdown?"

"Everything is splendid, sir."

Not taking Peter at his word, the two leaders of the wagon train completed a quick inspection of the wagon and the oxen's harness.

"Yep, looks to be fine. Don't forget to keep the axles greased." The Major tipped his hat once again, "Ma'am."

"Major?" Gertie called out.

"Yes?"

"The two wagons that were left behind at the river, wasn't that rather cruel? I mean, isn't the whole purpose in hiring you to solicit your assistance with such troubles?"

"Well, yes, Missus, ah, Berg, you are correct on both accounts. However, consider that everyone in the train is dependent upon my judgment and assistance to get them to Oregon. Make no mistake about it, this is a very difficult venture. Cruel as it may seem, crossing the Blue River is a test to separate the men from the boys. By this I mean, if a wagon team is not strong enough to complete the river crossing, then there is no chance they will live to see Oregon. Continuing to coddle them will only decrease the chances of everyone else. Thus, we weed them out while they are still close enough to Independence to get back."

"I see. I do understand, but it seems rather cruel to simply abandon them."

"Oh, I'm not so heartless. I left a wrangler to watch over them. One of the wagons did return to Independence. I will send his money back to him. The other is still on the trail. I expect they will be here in another hour."

"Thank you for telling me. I feel much better knowing this."

"Yes, ma'am, but don't tell the others. I prefer them to think of me as a cold, heartless bastard." The Major winked.

* * *

Fort Union, Northwest Wilderness

"Look after things. I'll be back in a couple weeks." Edgar Millar gave his final instructions to his new partners, Alistair and Corbin McKinsey.

Corbin had not been able to produce the fifty dollars Edgar had insisted was the amount needed to buy half of the trading post business. Together, the two brothers had come up with the money. Edgar had scribbled out a partnership agreement granting them half ownership in the trading post. The brothers had made their marks. Edgar was sure they couldn't read or write. However, the document was as legitimate as he could make it.

The three men had worked together packing the hides, which had been collected during the previous summer and fall, and cleaned during the winter. The hides were loaded into light, open craft called Mackinaw boats used by fur traders on the inland rivers and lakes. These would be floated down the Missouri River as soon as the ice broke. Edgar frequently told them about the scheduled trip to Independence, Missouri, to sell the hides and to purchase another supply of trade goods. He had droned on about the complexity of the transaction. He had told them of the need for the two men to guard their stockpile of goods and money while he was gone. "This hundred dollars is all the money we have. Guard it with your life," he had told them. The money was the brother's fifty dollars and another fifty which had previously belonged to Bart Adams. Edgar was willing to sacrifice this amount to ensure the two potential murderers would trust him for a little while longer.

The Mackinaw boats could float down the river anytime it was not ice bound. However, they could only go downriver. The steamboats could navigate upriver, but they could only travel during the spring when the water level was at its highest. Occasionally, the steamboats traveled further upstream, but Fort Union was essentially the end of the line for civilization. Therefore, it was a time of jubilation when the steamboat, St. Ange arrived.

The steamboat had arrived the tenth day of May with a fresh crop of young men to try their hand at fur trapping and buffalo hunting. Additionally, it brought up a standard shipment of food for the settlement, and a stash of rifles, trinkets, and other goods to be traded with the Indians. Edgar had paid for these with half of the Mackinaw boats loaded with hides. The other half of the hides would be sold in Independence to pay for the load of supplies for the steamboat's second and final trip of the year in late June.

Edgar bid farewell to the two murderous brothers and boarded the steamboat for the trip south. He breathed a sigh of relief when the steam whistle blew, the side paddlewheel churned the water, and the dock lines were cast off. Edgar turned his back on the fur trade business and faced his future downriver. With the sum total of his meager belongings wrapped in a buffalo skin, twenty ten-dollar gold pieces tucked in his money belt, his Bowie knife sheathed on his belt, and Bart Adams' Hawken rifle in his hand, Edgar was eager to return to the warmth of Missouri. It had been a year since he had truly been *warm*. The riverboat picked up speed, rounded the bend, and Edgar Millar's experience in Fort Union became nothing more than a memory.

"Aye, Mr. Millar, it's a bit chilly out. Da ya care to come inside for a nip?" The captain of the boat, Joe La Barge, was no stranger to Edgar.

"Thank you, don't mind if I do." Stepping into the protection of the wheelhouse, Edgar accepted the whiskey bottle from the Captain and took a warming swig. "How long before we can be taking hot baths in Independence?" he asked, after wiping his mouth on his sleeve.

"Nary a minute more than seven days, the Good Lord willing." Captain La Barge took a swig from the bottle. "We made the trip up from St. Louis in only twenty-six days. Fastest run ever." He passed the bottle back to Edgar.

"I plan on jumping ship and heading to California. I hear they found gold there, and I aim to get me some." Edgar spoke the truth, though he did not plan on actually panning for gold. He planned on establishing his own trading post for the miners. As with the buffalo hunters, there was easy money to be had in selling them supplies. He would leave the hard mining work to others.

"Indeed, but Bellevue is the best place to join the Oregon Trail. It's a hundred miles closer to California and we'll be there in only six days. Also, you don't have to cross the Kaw River like you do if you jump off at Independence."

"That so? Am I too late in the season? The wagon trains will be leaving Independence any day now. I've yet to get a rig."

"A man like you won't have any trouble. You could strike out on your own and catch up with a train. Sign on as a scout and get them to haul yer vittles. You speak injun, don't you?"

Edgar contemplated this idea, and nodded. "I speak a little of some injun from different tribes. Picked it up trading with 'em. I will get off at Bellevue. Traveling from there sounds like a good idea."

Edgar took a final pull from the whiskey bottle and handed it back to the captain. Joe corked it and returned his attention to the twisting, treacherous river. Edgar left him to find a spot to unroll his bed in the warm interior of the salon. There was no shortage of heat aboard a steamboat.

CHAPTER FIVE

June 1, 1848
Bellevue, Indian Territory

In the early morning hours, the steamboat St. Ange approached Council Bluffs, Iowa. This stop was necessary to obtain more coal for the fire which kept the boiler full of steam to power the boat. Council Bluffs was where the explorers, Lewis and Clark had first met with the Ote Indian tribe in 1804. A settlement of one sort or another had existed in the area since then. On the eastern side of the Missouri River, the town of Kanesville provided coal and supplies for the river traffic. The area had originally been settled by the Mormons, but by 1848 most of them had migrated westward, across the Missouri.

Once the boat was secured to the dock, Edgar Millar took the opportunity of the stillness of the boat to pen a letter to his mother:

Dearest Ma,

It is my prayer that this letter finds you well and in good spirits as am I. It is with regret that I have been unable to write until now. Let me briefly tell you of my travels to date.

After departing Pittsburg, I made my way westward to the Ohio River, where I joined the crew of a keelboat taking cargo down the Ohio to the Mississippi River. At Paducah, Kentucky, I had the good fortune to crew upon one of the new steamboats traveling upriver on the Mississippi to St. Louis. I did not stay long in that busy metropolis before I changed to a boat heading westward on the Missouri River. It was at this time that I met the most interesting mountain man, Bart Adams. He traveled with our boat to Independence, Missouri. It was indeed lucky for me that he did for that is where I had the unfortunate experience of being waylaid by thieves. Mr. Adams attended to my wounds. Not only was I wounded and all my money stolen but I also missed the steamboat's return journey to St Louis. It was under the guidance of kind providence that Mr. Adams offered me a job.

It was not only as the result of my great indebtedness to him, but also because of my growing respect, that I traveled with him to the farthest reaches of the Northwest Wilderness. We finally stopped at a place called Fort Union. Mr. Adams operated an Indian trading post there and I worked for him for a year. I learned so much from him about trading with the Indians and trappers.

It is with great sadness I say that Mr. Adams was murdered by a thieving scum named Alistair McKinsey. Following my friend's death, I was forced to flee in fear for my own life. All these afflictions were undoubtedly set upon me for some good end. I surely have had my share of misfortune, but you know that I never give up. Never give up for tis wiser and better to hope than fall into despair.

And in hopes that this day will usher in a bright future, I am back aboard a sturdy steamboat on the Missouri River. I am at this juncture continuing west across the new territories to California. I have heard that gold has been found there.
Your loving son,
Edgar
June 1, 1848

While it had only been two years, it seemed like a lifetime ago when Edgar had come to blows with his father. While this argument had been the cause of his hasty departure, he had difficulty remembering what they had been fighting about. The tensions between father and son had arisen originally over marriage and career choices. It grew to the point that it took little to incite an argument. Regretting past events, he added at the bottom of the paper:

Give my warm regards to Papa. I am sorry that I could not fulfill his wish for me, and marry for money. The man who marries for money may better his worldly condition, but this is a hard fate. You spoke the truth when you said that I care not for such things. No, give me a woman who possesses the qualities to make a man happy, though poverty be her lot. With such I could pass through the world in happiness. And so, the life of a lawyer is not mine. I am sorry for the financial straits that my action has cast the family into. At my earliest opportunity, I will send you money.

After closing the letter to his mother and addressing it, he took a second piece of paper and drafted a contract. This contract authorized Captain La Barge to sell his hides and purchase supplies to be taken back to Fort Union. Edgar intended to fulfill his obligations to the McKinsey brothers. In exchange for his services, La Barge was to retain ten percent of the value of the hides. He attached the list of the requested supplies.

At noon and ten miles further south, Captain La Barge stopped the boat close ashore at Bellevue.

"Joe," Edgar addressed the Captain, "may I burden you with seeing that this letter reaches my mother in Pittsburgh?"

"Certainly."

"And I wish to commission you to trade my hides and see to the supplies for the McKinsey brother in Fort Union." Edgar showed him the contract and he signed it. "Be wary in your dealings with them two. I've no proof, but I'm certain Alistair murdered Bart Adams."

With a final nod, Edgar Millar climbed overboard and waded ashore.

Bellevue had been established in 1822 as the only fur trading post on the west side of the Missouri River. The post was located where the Platte River joined the Missouri. The original intention had been to establish riverboat traffic westward on the Platte River. However, this river proved to be a mile wide and an inch deep. Even the Indians carried their canoes instead of attempting to navigate the waterway. With the addition of a ferry crossing the Missouri River, Oregon bound settlers could now stage their departure closer to their destination than at Independence.

Wading ashore, Edgar made a beeline towards the largest building in the town, a two-story, wooden structure which housed a combination hotel, saloon, and bathhouse.

"How much for a bath?" he inquired.

"Ten cents," the clerk replied.

"How much for fresh, clean hot water?" He had not had a real tub bath in a year, and he did not want someone else's used water.

The clerk eyed him, and answered, "That'll be four bits."

Edgar added a second quarter-dollar for a shave and a haircut. Striping his clothes off, but carefully keeping his belongings in sight and his bowie knife under the water in the tub, he washed away a year of buffalo stench. He laid back and soaked while a young woman shaved off his beard and cut his hair. Afterwards, he went into the saloon for a double shot of whiskey followed by a beer.

With his needs for a hot bath and a shot of red-eye satiated, he turned to the next item on his mental list. He studied the women seated under the stairs. Given that they were attired in only their undergarments, he had no doubts as to their profession. Their bare feet advertised that they wore nothing under their meager clothing. While continuing to sip his beer, someone tugged on his sleeve. Turning, he saw the woman who had shaved him. She smiled, but said nothing as she reached for his hand.

Edgar allowed her to lead him up the stairs. Once inside her room, he placed a dollar on the small table beside her bed. Slowly, she undressed him. Edgar had not known which woman would invite him upstairs, but he had expected the transaction. In preparation, he had bundled his money belt in the folds of his buffalo hide.

"Where did you get these?" she asked, holding up his doeskin shirt and buckskin trousers.

"An Indian woman named Wyalla made them for me."

"She is very skilled. Is she Pawnee?" She studied the decorative stitching.

The woman was obviously part Indian and Edgar guessed her to be half Pawnee. "No, Blackfoot." He did not bother to tell her that Wyalla was dead.

"You are from very far away."

"Yes, from a place that is always cold and now I want to get warm."

"I will warm you," she seductively said, in Pawnee. Edgar spoke a few words in several of the Indian dialects, but he was not proficient in Pawnee. However, he had understood her. He would have understood her had she spoken Chinese.

"Show me how warm I can be," he responded in Lakota. While the native language of the Sioux, most Indians understood more Lakota than he understood Pawnee.

When he was naked, she tucked him into bed like a child. He watched as she disrobed. Unlike the other women in the saloon, she had been fully clothed. Edgar's excitement mounted with each article she removed. At the conclusion of her performance, she stood before him unclothed. She allowed his admiration of her tawny body with unashamed grace. Looking into his eyes, she slipped into bed. Once beneath the faded quilt, she wrapped her warm, smooth body around his.

"Are you warm now, Mr. Blackfoot?" She continued speaking Lakota.

"Almost," he sighed.

Placing his hand on her left shoulder, he gently rolled her onto her back. She wrapped her arms and legs around him and held on tight as their bodies intertwined and their scents mingled. What began slowly became a ride as wild as either had experienced for quite some time.

When they had both exhausted their need, Edgar held her warm body close to his. Relishing the steady rhythm of her heartbeat, he fell asleep.

* * *

The woman was still snug in his arms when the first rays of sunlight awoke him. Edgar lifted her chin and kissed her good morning. The sleeping beauty opened her eyes and smiled. It had been a night well spent for both. With the beginning of the day, he focused on his journey.

With a slight hesitation and speaking in English, Edgar asked, "Do you know if there are any wagon trains heading west?"

"They are gone one week now. More settlers and wagons will come soon. You are going to Oregon?"

Edgar was not concerned that he had missed the first wagon train, and he had no interest in waiting for another to assemble.

"Do you know where I can buy a horse and saddle for a fair price?" he asked, ignoring her question.

"Yes, my brother has a horse. I will take you there. He will be fair. And a saddle too, I'm sure."

Edgar was concerned that she might not be telling the truth, but he had no better idea.

"How can I trust that he will be fair?"

Her eyes gleamed as she alluringly caressed his broad, hairy chest. "I will show you."

She slipped from his arms and scooted down under the covers. She knelt between his thighs, teasing him with her teeth. His hands caressed her hair. She looked up at him and flashed him a flirtatious, but wicked smile.

"Do you trust me?" she whispered.

Groaning, Edgar lay back and with a full measure of trust surrendered himself to her.

*　*　*

The Indian man that the woman indicated to be her brother bore no resemblance to her. His bronze skin was a deeper hue than her tawny complexion and his broad, angular nose looked nothing like her round, button nose. If they were siblings, they shared only one parent. However, he began to dicker fairly when Edgar addressed him in Lakota. Soon, they reached what Edgar thought was a fair price. The chocolate stallion with white feet that he bought was a magnificent animal—healthy and strong. The saddle he purchased was worn, but he examined all the leather straps and found no cracks or undue wear.

"Mr. Blackfoot, want to take me with you? I can be your wife." The half-Indian woman asked.

Edgar mounted his new horse. "I'm sorry, but I cannot afford a wife right now." He gave her a second dollar. Following a quick kiss, he was gone. Neither knew the other's name and Edgar felt no regrets.

Edgar's last stop was at the trading post were he bought a sack of hardtack, a slab of bacon, coffee, and other supplies. The hardtack was thin bread, slowly baked until it was rock hard. As long as it was kept dry, this would remain edible for months. However, it was only edible once mixed with grease, or in a soup. The heavily salted bacon would also keep for a long time. While it might slowly spoil, the rancid portion could be trimmed away.

While not enough to get him to California, he figured this food would be sufficient to get him to Fort John if he augmented it with fresh deer meat from time to time. Fort John was a trading post located at the junction of the Laramie and Platte Rivers, the halfway point along the Oregon Trail. However, he hoped he would catch up with the wagon train in less than two weeks. He hoped Captain La Barge had been correct and that he could sign on as a scout. Trading wasn't all his former friend and partner had taught him. Edgar's final purchase was a Colt Walker 44-caliber revolver.

While on the north side of the Platte River, Edgar nudged his spurs against the horse and directed the stallion westward. The river made a large looping bend to the north, but he would cross the river and head due west to make better time. In a few days he would again intersect the river and follow it upstream, continuing west. The wagon trains typically covered twenty miles a day; he would have to double that to catch them. Edgar and his unnamed steed had a hard ride ahead of them. At this point, Edgar was grateful for the used saddle; he would not have the agony of breaking in a new one as he set off on a two thousand mile ride.

Following the Oregon Trail was unexpectedly easy. The hundred or so wagons ahead of him, along with the thousand or so animal hooves, had churned the earth for a twenty-five yard wide swath. There was not one pair of wagon-wheel ruts, but several ruts which ran in parallel, creating the wide path. Occasionally, one set of ruts became too deep in the soft, moist soil and was abandoned. He could see the chaos of hoof prints and wagon ruts as the abandoned softer route was angled back onto the harder ground.

On the third day of his travels, Edgar encountered the Platte River and his first turn-back. A weary family of four had abandoned the journey and decided to head home. Edgar removed his hat and nodded to the woman riding in the wagon.

"How far ahead is the train?" he asked the man walking beside the oxen.

"We turned back three days ago, so less than a hundred miles, I reckon," the man replied.

Edgar nodded again to them, and continued westward.

* * *

Along the Oregon Trail

The first leg of Gertie's trip to Oregon passed easily. She was surprised to discover that the Oregon Trail was not a single, marked roadway. Rather, it was a wide swath of land with hundreds of wagons heading west through the waist-high prairie grass. The wagons within the organized trains remained close together as they passed and were passed by individual groups of three and four wagons.

They stopped briefly each hour to water the oxen. To keep the beasts satiated, the Berg's wagon had two water barrels strapped to its sides. When possible they camped near streams and the barrels were refilled by a bucket brigade. Major Jamison said that, as the teams become more used to the travel, the stops to water the animals would be less frequent. The teams were tame and easily coaxed into pulling the wagons at a walking pace mile after mile, but they could not be forced to move faster. Additionally, if they became too thirsty, they would bolt and follow their noses to the nearest watering hole.

With the passage of time, the groups of settlers drifted farther apart as they traveled at their own pace and chose slightly different routes. The prairie soil along the Kaw River was soft, and heavy wagons sank several inches into the dirt making them sluggish. After their second day on the trail, Gertie began to see where people had abandoned some of their property. Heavy, unnecessary items such as a table and cupboard, cast-iron stove, and even a wooden bed frame with its featherbed began to litter the prairie. She convinced Peter to pick up two chairs so they would have something besides the ground to sit upon while they camped. She wished she could ask for the featherbed, but they simply had no room for it.

Major Jamison paid a group of Indians to ferry the wagons in his train across the Kaw River. The band of natives had a flat log raft and took the fifty wagons across the river one at a time. While all four of the organized wagon trains paid for the ferry, most of the unorganized travelers lacked the funds for this, and they continued westward in search of shallow water where they could make the crossing.

"Crossing here," the Major had explained, "will allow us to take a more direct route to the Platte River, which will save us many days of travel time."

While the bulk of the pioneers continued west along the southern shore of the Kaw River, Major Jamison's wagon train turned northwest. They crossed many smaller rivers, and the beds of these were churned into muddy quagmires by the enumerable wagons and animal hooves. Often Indians gathered to watch as the travelers crossed and they swarmed around wagons which became stuck in the mud. This was not done in a menacing way but with a friendly display of humor. Through sign language and broken English these Indians negotiated a price to help free the stuck wagons. The price could be a few pennies or some item in trade. The sense of good will and the much needed help made the crossings safer and easier. Peter and Gertie were fortunate in that they did not need the help.

The Major established a pattern where his wife and a scout would ride ahead of the train in the morning. They would go about fifteen miles and locate a grazing area suitable for a midday break and meal for the train's pioneers. She boiled up several pots of beans and baked cornbread in Dutch ovens. When the wagon train caught up with them, each family augmented the meal with their own bacon or wild game meat. In this way, minimal time was lost when they stopped for lunch. Once the rest and meal were completed, the pair would ride ahead again to find a campsite for the night.

The wagon train traveled in two parallel rows of twenty-five wagons each. Their livestock grazed between the rows. At midday, they stopped and unhitched the oxen to allow them to graze while the emigrants ate their lunch. At night, the wagons were pulled closer together and the ends of the two rows were closed to form a giant ellipse. The wranglers allowed the livestock to graze while the evening meal was prepared and eaten. With the approach of darkness, the livestock were herded inside the ellipse for the night. Most of the people camped in tents on the outside of the curved formation.

Gertie observed that Martha had been mistaken in her assumption of companionship. The four wagon trains were probably within a dozen miles of each other, but she had no idea where the Mormon train was located. After the first few days, she had not seen another wagon train. She was saddened by the lack of Martha's conversation. Gertie had enjoyed her and her family.

The further north of the Kaw River that they traveled, the more flat and featureless the prairie became. Without any trees, they used buffalo chips for cooking fuel. The buffalo migrated across the plains in herds which numbered in the thousands and their sun-dried waste was flammable. She had been surprised the first time she saw the buffalo poop burned because there was no bad odor; it was perfect for cooking meals. The buffalo turds were easy to find as they traveled. Strange the things she learned. Gertie spent a large portion of her day walking along beside the wagon train collecting this fuel into a large basket. She enjoyed straying far from the wagons. From a distance, they did appear to be sailing ships traversing a sea of grass. She was reminded of her trip across the Atlantic Ocean as a child. The gentle rolling hills were the waves of this ocean and the tips of the grass swaying in the wind resembled the foam on the wave crests. Completing the metaphor was the seasickness that many of the people experienced while riding in the wagons as they tumbled along the prairie.

Sweeping her arms across the tall grass, she wondered why they didn't simply stop here and claim this land. However, she knew the answer. The government had reserved it for the sole use of the Indians. Occasionally a buffalo was killed and butchered to add to the supplies. Often the meat would be cooked in the morning and packed away for the midday stop. Gertie had no idea if the government or the

Indians approved of the hunting or not, but given the thousands of buffalo that they saw, she spent little time thinking about it.

While Gertie never saw the Indians on the plains, area tribes knew where the wagon train was. Several Indians would always be found waiting for them at the river crossings. These people did not speak English as the Indians had weeks earlier and they refused money. In exchange for their help, the locals bartered for the trade goods. They had an affinity for anything made of cotton fabric. Gertie watched one man exchange a bag of flour for one Indian's assistance. The native promptly opened the bag and dumped the flour on the ground, keeping only the cloth bag. Eventually the train moved further west than the range of the Indians and their assistance disappeared. The pioneers were forced to complete the crossings with only the help of their fellow travelers. However, they had garnered the skills required for this trip west.

"Another week and we will cross the South Platte River," Major Jamison said at their nightly campfire meeting. "We'll ease up and rest there before following the river west."

A few miles into the trip on the next day, they prepared to cross a small river at the bottom of a deep ravine. There were no Indians to help them. The wagons had to approach the fast moving waterway by angling down the ravine wall. This experience was new and dangerous.

The Berg's wagon was halfway across the river when the wagon behind them, still partway up the hillside, sank down in the mud. The man was insufficiently experienced with oxen and did not possess the courage and strength to control his team by whip and tone of command. The fearful, baffled oxen turned to climb back up the hill, the wagon flipped onto its side. Bound to the yoke, the oxen also rolled over. With nothing anchoring the rig, it slid down to the river. The entire assembly floated down upon Gertie and Peter. Peter mercilessly whipped their oxen to urge them to cross faster.

Gertie watched in horror as the wagons collided.

CHAPTER SIX

June 14, 1848
Fate Intervenes

Edgar was startled awake. His horse snorted angrily. His front legs were hobbled, but still the beast pounded the ground. Instinctively, Edgar reached under the buffalo hide for the butt of his revolver. Grasping it, he opened his eyes to the pre-dawn darkness. His chocolate stallion whinnied and dug his rear hooves into the soft earth. Edgar looked upward at his horse standing a few yards away. The wary animal kicked and sprayed dirt behind him. Edgar followed the horse's stare to the horizon.

The Indian was silhouetted against the pink sky. In the darkness, Edgar could discern no details of his visitor, but the stallion was distinctly annoyed by the invader, or more likely, his pony. Climbing from his bedding, Edgar stood and stared at the Indian on horseback. He stared back. With the rising sun behind him, Edgar judged the Indian could clearly see him and his camp in the thicket of cottonwood trees. Edgar picked up the Hawken rifle from beside his buffalo hide bedding. While not holding it in a threatening manner, he allowed the Indian to see the weapon as he propped it up against a tree.

As expected, upon seeing the rifle the Indian turned and rode down the backside of the hill. However, he left something behind. He had stabbed his spear into the ground and there was something waving on its end, like a flag.

Sensing a need to get moving before the Indian returned with his friends, Edgar skipped his coffee and breakfast. Hastily, he packed his bedroll and saddled the stallion. Mounting his horse, Edgar pointed him westward, along the Platte River and away from where the Indian had left his mysteriously waving flag.

What in tarnation is that?

Halting, Edgar glanced over his shoulder at the flag on the crest of the hill. Wondering why the Indian would leave his spear behind, Edgar turned and urged his horse up the hill. Slowly, expecting a dozen Indians to be hiding on the other side, he rode up to the spot where the Indian had been standing. As he approached, he observed the flag was some sort of cloth, and that it was yellow.

Where could an Indian get yellow cloth?

Edgar released the strap holding his revolver in its holster and cradled the Hawken in the crook of his arm. Slowing the stallion to a walking pace, he crested the hill. The Indian waited for him at the bottom—alone. Edgar pulled the spear from the ground and examined the cloth. It was a woman's yellow sunbonnet. He pulled the bonnet free from the spear and stuffed it under his shirt.

The Indian trotted his horse a dozen yards to the west, stopped, and turned to face Edgar. In the brighter light, Edgar could see he was Pawnee and they were generally a peaceful Indian tribe.

"All right," he said to his horse with an assuring pat on his neck, "I'll bite."

He followed the Indian west, the direction he had wanted to go anyway.

Once Edgar made it clear he would follow, the Indian urged his spotted pony into a trot. Cautiously, Edgar remained twenty-five yards behind as the two men rode a mile westward.

On the top of a hill, the Indian came to a halt and stared down at a small river. Edgar brought his horse to a stop several yards away, and followed the man's gaze. In a cottonwood grove on the riverbank, two bodies were sprawled in the grass.

Edgar scanned the sky. Seeing no buzzards, he concluded that the two victims had not been dead long. The carrion eaters had not yet found them.

Edgar saw a splash of yellow; the color matched the sunbonnet. He reasoned there was no motivation for the Indian to kill the settlers, and then guide him to them. Nonetheless, Edgar kept the Indian's spear as he trotted his horse down to the dead couple. Approaching, he noted the pasty-white body of a nude man. The second corpse was a fully clothed woman. She wore a yellow blouse which matched the sunbonnet. Cold remnants of a campfire were visible, no cooking utensils or other supplies.

Edgar dismounted. The corpse of the young man was completely naked and lying on his back. The Indian dismounted as well, but kept his distance. The dead man had a bullet hole in the center of his forehead. There were powder burns on his face, but no exit wound. While some Indians did have rifles, very few had pistols. The power of a rifle shot would have created an exit wound, therefore Edgar concluded, this man had been shot with a pistol. The powder burns indicated the assailant had been no more than two feet away. Indians routinely took the clothing of their victims, and Edgar reasoned he had been stripped to make the murder look like an Indian attack.

But why not strip the woman?

The fully clothed woman lay face down and Edgar reached to roll her over. As he moved her, she sucked in a gasping breath. Her hands, face, and blouse were stained with blood, but he could find no wounds. She continued to breathe, but did not awaken.

Edgar retrieved his canteen and tore a strip of cloth from her apron. He gently washed the blood from her face and hands. Slowly, her eyes opened. When they focused on Edgar, she screamed.

"You're safe now," he said and held her tight as she struggled. "You're safe," he repeated. "Are you injured?"

She sucked in a few short breaths and stopped struggling. She looked up into his face. "Who are you?"

Edgar tossed his hat aside so she could see his face. "My name is Edgar Millar. I've just come upon you. Are you injured?" He released her and she sat up.

"No, no, I'm not." Her eyes drifted to the Indian standing by the horses and she shrieked again.

"He won't hurt you. He's with me. Actually, he saved your life." Her eyes shifted to the dead man. Edgar regretted not having covered the body. Had he known she had been alive, he would have.

"That was my husband." She began to sob.

Edgar touched her arm to return her focus to him. "And what is your name?"

She wiped her face to compose herself. "Gertie, that is Gertrude Berg."

Stepping away from where she sat, he addressed the required task. Out of respect for the dead and the living, he needed to bury the remains before wild animals desecrated it.

He spoke to Mrs. Berg, "Rest here a bit and collect yer-self."

Edgar untied his bedroll from his horse and placed it over Mr. Berg's body. Pulling his Bowie knife from his belt, he began to dig a hole to bury the man. The big blade easily churned up the soft earth, but he had to scoop it out of the hole with his hands. After a few moments, the Indian knelt to help using his small knife. Edgar recognized the type of cheap, iron knives that he had traded with the Indians at Fort Union. These were quick to dull and rust, and had to be replaced frequently. He studied the Indian up close for the first time. He was lean and young, in his late teens, with coal black hair and eyes.

"Here, you dig while I fix us something to eat." Edgar spoke Lakota to him, but he gave no sign that he understood. Edgar handed him the big, steel blade and gestured for him to continue digging.

As he moved past the new widow, Edgar noticed she was still quietly crying. He relit the campfire the couple had built before the deadly attack. Using water from his canteen, he heated his coffee pot while he ground a handful of coffee beans with the butt of his revolver. In his frying pan, he used his parry knife to slice six thick strips from his slab of bacon. As the grease sizzled, he tossed in a half dozen chips of hardtack to soak up the grease and soften.

When the Indian had dug a three foot deep hole, long enough and wide enough to hold the man's body, Edgar walked over and stopped him. Together they gently laid Peter's body to rest and covered his remains with the loose soil. They tamped the mounded dirt as tightly as they could. Edgar gathered fallen wood from the cottonwood thicket which was thick enough for the final task. He cut two sticks and fashioned a cross to mark the grave.

Returning to the campfire, Edgar scooped out a third of the food from the pan onto his one and only plate and poured coffee into his only tin cup. He took them to Mrs. Berg.

"Here, you need to eat something."

Gertie looked at him with unfocused, far-away eyes, but took the plate and cup. Edgar quickly ate a second third of the food straight out of the pan, using a piece of dry hardtack as a spoon. He sipped coffee directly from the pot. Finished, he handed the pan to the Indian. The bronze man's stony face eyed the mixture and he sniffed it. Mimicking Edgar, the man ate. He smiled and Edgar figured the young brave had never eaten bacon or any pork before now.

Edgar studied the ground where the dead man had been. A few yards from the fire, he found wagon ruts and the hoof prints from two oxen and a horse. The tracks of the wagon wheels came from the west, but disappeared into the river.

"Mrs. Berg, what happened here?" he asked.

"We turned around," she spoke barely above a whisper, assuming he would know what 'turned around' meant. She stared at the grave. "We camped here for the night. I went off into the trees to... to do what was necessary. A man rode up on horseback. I saw him, but was detained in my approach of the campsite." She paused to look into Edgar's eyes to determine if she needed to explain more. Seeing he understood what she had been doing, she continued, "I didn't see exactly what happened, but I heard the gunshot. I hid in the brush and watched while he took Peter's money belt. But then, he took all of Peter's clothes off. Then he tied his horse to the back of our wagon and took it across the river." She pointed along the direction of the tracks. "I ran to Peter. I held him in my arms, but there was nothing I could do." She sobbed and Edgar comforted her.

"It was a white man?"

"Yes," she turned to look at the Indian.

"We best be on our way, ma'am," he said to Gertie, and packed up his kit.

"Where? Where are we going?"

"West, ma'am. We'll catch up with another wagon train and see what can be done for you."

She turned toward the eastern horizon and worked her jaw as though considering her options. Of course, there were none. Sighing, she stood and walked to the grave. She knelt and prayed.

"Dear God, accept this good man into your welcoming arms." She stood, stiffened her spine and turned toward the stranger. "All right, I'll come with you," she said.

Edgar thought her comment to be ridiculous considering the circumstances, but he said nothing. He lifted her up, to sit sideways in the stallion's saddle. The chocolate stud was skittish at the woman's approach. However, he quickly quieted as Edgar mounted behind her and wrapped his arms around her to hold the horse's reins. Pinned between his chest and the pommel of the saddle, the slender woman held onto the saddle horn as Edgar urged the big horse westward.

Surprisingly, the Indian followed.

"You're dressed like him, but you're not an Indian." Gertie observed his deerskin clothing, apparently for the first time. "Do you live with them?"

"I lived among the Indians for the past year, but now I'm heading to California." Edgar saw no reason to explain further. "How long ago did you turn back?"

"It was yesterday. There was an accident crossing the river the day before. A man drowned and our wagon was toppled. Our food supply was lost. Major Jamison, the wagonmaster, forced us to turn back. He said we could follow the river to the Platte, and then to Bellevue where we could resupply. Peter and I intended to join another train." She paused for a moment. "Major Jamison gave us back our money, but that man—the one who killed Peter—stole it all. He stole everything." She pressed her face into Edgar's chest trying to smother the sobs which welled up unbidden.

After several minutes Gertie ceased sobbing, readjusted her position across the saddle, and dried her eyes.

"I'm very sorry about your husband."

She inhaled deeply and released the breath in a long slow sigh. "I didn't really know him."

"What do you mean?"

"It was an arranged marriage. I've only known him for two months. He was a good man and had the makings of a good husband. I am sorry that he is dead." She studied the Indian and changed the subject. "Is he going to California with you?"

"I don't rightly know. I fed him and, like a lost puppy, I can't seem to shake him. He's Pawnee and I don't speak their language. I don't know how far he plans to follow us." Edgar briefly related the story of how the Indian had led him to her. "Here, this is yours." He remembered the sunbonnet and pulled it out from under his shirt.

She tied the bonnet in place upon her head. Gertie used her right hand to grip the saddle horn. She struggled to find a comfortable balance, and for a moment, she put her other arm around his waist. Edgar took his left arm and placed it across her body resting his hand on her right hip, intruding upon her person as little as possible. Seeming to find comfort in the position, she leaned into his shoulder. Gently grasped his arm and steadied herself.

Urgently needing to find shelter for the exhausted woman, Edgar spurred the big horse into a trot. She fell asleep with the side of her face lying against his chest. At midday, the young Indian shouted several unrecognizable words and woke her. She and Edgar watched as the Indian shook his spear in the air and peeled away to ride south. She sat upright to watch him gallop into the distance.

"Where's he going?" she asked, in a confused, sleepy voice.

"I've no idea. Back to his home, I guess. While I did appreciate his help, I'm relieved he chose to leave us. He seemed friendly enough, but ya never know what an Indian might do."

At dusk, Edgar located a wagon train camped for the night. He smelled the campfires before he spotted it. The welcoming smells of frying meat, corn pone, and biscuits drifted toward them. His stomach grumbled.

* * *

As they approached the camp, a wrangler rode up to them and halted his horse crosswise, blocking the path. Gertie recognized the Mormon man and spoke before he could challenge them.

"Good day, Mr. Rees, are Abram and Martha Smoot here?" she asked of the wrangler.

"Aye, and who are you two?"

"It's me, Gertie Berg. Do you remember me from Independence? I'm a friend of Martha Smoot. I was with Major Jamison's train, but I got separated. This is Mr. Millar. He found me." Gertie took a breath to stop her rambling.

"Yes, ma'am," Rees said, and examined Edgar with a cold stare.

"I'm Edgar Millar. May I speak with the wagonmaster?" Edgar introduced himself.

"Aye, follow me."

Edgar and Gertie followed him into the camp.

"You know these people?" Edgar asked of her.

"Yes, they were camped next to us in Independence. They were behind us after we crossed the Kaw River."

As was the practice of Major Jamison's train, the Mormon wagons were parked in an elliptical shape.

"Martha!" Gertie spotted her friend and shouted to her. Edgar dismounted and held her hips to steady her as she jumped down from the horse.

"Gertie!" Martha hugged her and examined the blood staining her blouse. "What has happened to you?"

"It was horrible. Peter was murdered." She sobbed for a moment while Martha hugged her. Composing herself, she said "A man shot him and stole everything we had. Mr. Millar here saved me." She wiped her eyes before introducing everyone, and related the story of the disaster crossing the river and how she and Peter had turned back.

"Come, you will stay with us," Abram said. "We thank you, kind sir, for your assistance." He shook Edgar's hand. "If there's any service we can perform for you, you need only ask."

"What's the matter here?" A pudgy, older, bow-legged man approached them. While he wore his beard in the Mormon fashion, it was pure white.

"Mr. Hatch," Abram introduced them, "this is Mrs. Gertie Berg and Mr. Millar. Mr. Hatch is our wagonmaster."

Edgar held out his hand. "Edgar Millar, sir." Edgar continued with a synopsis of their story.

"Mrs. Berg, you say your husband was murdered? Did you know the assailant?" Hatch asked.

"No, but I did see some of him. He was about thirty years old with dark brown hair, but no beard. Tall and lanky, rather like Mr. Millar. He had a scar on his chin and a game-leg—his left leg. He gathered up all of our belongings and took our wagon."

"I'm very sorry, ma'am, but there is no law west of Missouri. If we had the man in our grasp, we would hang him. However, there is no means to track him down and punish him."

Gertie silently nodded.

"Mr. Hatch," Abram interrupted, "Mrs. Berg is welcome to stay with us."

Hatch nodded and Edgar added, "Sir, I need employment for myself. I was educated as a lawyer in Pittsburgh, Pennsylvania, but most recently I've been a hunter and trader with the Indians. I can scout for you, and help you when dealing with the Indians."

"A lawyer dressed as an Indian," he chuckled. "Much obliged, Mr. Millar, but I'm afraid that I can't take you on. You're welcome to stay the night. However, in the morning I expect you will be moving on."

Hatch turned on his heel and walked away.

After a moment of stunned silence, Abram said, "Please, Mr. Millar, have supper with us and you can camp here." He swallowed and added, "I apologize for his rudeness. I don't understand why he would not allow you to stay."

"It's quite all right, Mr. Smoot. It is pure economics. He has a full staff and a limited amount of supplies. He sees me as an unnecessary extra mouth to feed," Edgar said.

Edgar spread out his buffalo bedding and helped Abram assemble a makeshift tent for Gertie. They draped canvas sheets along the sides of the wagon and made a pallet with a horse blanket. Gertie joined Martha in the wagon and, a few minutes later, reappeared wearing a clean white shirt tucked into her skirt.

"Mr. Millar, what will you do now?" Gertie asked as they ate.

"Oh, I expect I'll continue riding west. You say there are other wagon trains ahead?"

"Yes, four trains left Independence more or less together. I imagine they can't be more than a day or two ahead."

"Mrs. Berg?" He paused until she turned to him. "I'm sorry I can't take you east. I suppose that you want to return to your family. Perhaps another turn-back can be persuaded to take you."

"I will give that some thought, Mr. Millar. Truth be known, there is not much for me back in Cincinnati. At this moment the only thing I miss there is my soft bed and quiet room. My father essentially tossed me out and forced me to marry Mr. Berg. I doubt he would see me starve, but I would have to find some means to support myself. And, of course," she sighed, "I've no money. I've no means to travel east. Like it or not, my future now lies westward."

"Hmm, much the same for me. I'll be up early and gone in the morning. So, ma'am, I'll bid you a farewell tonight. You have my best wishes for a safe journey." He smiled and tipped his hat.

"Well, I'll turn in as well," Gertie said to Martha and Abram.

She crawled into her tent under the wagon. Lifting the flap, she watched as Edgar kicked off his boots, placed his hat over his revolver, and wrapped himself in the buffalo hide. Gertie watched him for a long moment. She watched the splashes of orange light from the campfire flames dance around him. He was tall and lean with firm muscles and a kind, attractive face. He was polite and had spoken to her so tenderly. He was so much that Peter had not been.

Gertie's thoughts of her dead husband were not meant to be cruel. Just honest. He was gone and that portion of her life was finished. With the future always uncertain, Gertie turned her thoughts to survival. She would face what was necessary to reach the west and begin a new life.

CHAPTER SEVEN

June 15, 1848
Indians

Gertie suffered a restless night of intermingled bad dreams. She dreamt of Peter and Indians and Mr. Millar in an incomprehensible collage. She woke up thinking of her rescuer, Edgar Millar, and wished she had given him a proper goodbye. He had saved her life. When she arose, she approached his horse, saddled and tied to the back of the wagon. The chocolate stallion snorted and stretched his neck toward her. She stroked its velvet nose and regretted she had nothing to feed it when it searched her palm for a treat.

There was no other sign of Mr. Millar.

Seeing no steaming pot beside the fire, Gertie asked of Martha, "Would you like me to prepare the coffee?"

Martha appeared startled. "Goodness no," she snorted. Seeing Gertie's perplexed expression, she added, "You mean, you don't know?"

"Know what?" Gertie asked.

"Don't you know, we Mormons don't drink coffee? Our bodies are a precious gift from God and He gave us laws to keep our bodies and minds healthy and strong. Such things as tobacco, alcohol, and coffee contain harmful substances which alter the ability to think."

"Yes, of course." Gertie certainly agreed alcohol impaired one's thinking. While coffee altered one's thinking, she found it a welcomed way to clear the head in the morning. "I'll learn to get along without it." Gertie sighed and yawned. "Do you mean to say that you have never tasted wine?"

Martha glanced over her shoulder to ensure their conversation was private. "Mr. Smoot and I were invited to a Protestant wedding once. I did sample the wine. I must say, I didn't care for it." She made a sour face. "Abram saw me drink it, and when we got home, I got quite the walloping." Her eyebrows shot up. "Not something I would do again, that's for sure."

Gertie did her best to conceal her astonishment and looked at her shoes. As she pondered, a rapidly approaching rider drew her attention. Mr. Rees rode up in a cloud of dust and drew his horse to a tight reigned halt. "Where is he?"

"Mr. Millar? I don't know," Gertie answered.

Rees stood tall in the stirrups and scanned the area. "That's his horse?"

"Yes."

"You," Rees shouted, seeing Edgar approaching from the brush along the riverbank, "Mr. Hatch wants to see you—directly."

Edgar grunted acknowledgement and mounted his horse. He gave no greeting to Gertie. She still wished to properly thank him and his seeming dismissal confused her. She took a few steps, following the men. The riders disappeared over a low hill. Determined to speak to Mr. Millar one last time, she lifted her skirt for a faster run and doggedly followed after them. Topping the rise, she froze.

The wagon train master's wife, Mrs. Hatch, was sitting on a buckboard wagon drawn by two horses. Beside her were four men on horseback: a scout, Hatch, Rees, and Edgar. Facing them, were ten Indians mounted on horseback. Three of whom carried rifles with the butts resting casually on their hips. The barrels pointed skyward, but the guns were readily accessed for immediate use.

"All right, Mr. Millar, you said you could negotiate with Indians. Go see what they want," Hatch commanded.

Edgar urged his nervous horse forward. Gertie noticed one of the Indians was the young man who had been with Edgar when he found her. As she stood staring, she noticed what she had been too preoccupied to see the previous day. The Indians weren't dressed at all like Mr. Millar. Edgar's clothes were fashioned from leather, but they were actual trousers and shirt. The Indian's leather clothing consisted of layers of smaller leather pieces. What looked like trousers were actually leggings, or chaps from his ankles to his hips. The two halves were tied together around his waist. Also around his bronzed trim waist were two swatches of leather, one in front and one in back. These flaps of rawhide formed something like a loincloth. He wore a vest and an earthen colored wrap similar to a cape tied around his neck to cover his shoulders and upper arms. The straight, long, flowing black hair was held out of his eyes by a tight band around his forehead. He wore a single, tall black feather placed in the band behind his head.

Gertie's eyes swept across the other natives and focused on the central man, the apparent leader of the band. This man sat tall on his spotted pony with an air of character and command. The realization that a primitive individual could carry such stature stunned her.

She watched while Edgar conversed with the leader of the Indians. He employed a combination of unintelligible words and hand gestures. The young one who had rescued her gave no sign of recognition. He remained as stoic and silent as the others atop their horses.

Edgar returned to Hatch. "They're some upset with you. This is their favorite hunting ground, but you've frightened away all the game, and now their women and children will go hungry."

"It's open land. It doesn't belong to anyone. We've as much right to be here as them," Hatch answered.

"They don't see it quite that way. Anyway, they seem to be willing to let the matter go. I expect they are not really all that angry; they just want their position understood. They've invited me to go with them and hunt somewhere else."

"Are you going to do it?"

"Well, if I decline, that might raise their ire... their anger toward you." Using his finger, Edgar stabbed the air between himself and Hatch.

Hatch studied him for a moment, and grunted. "All right, when you return from the hunt with your redskin friends, you can ride with us to Fort John, but that's it. There, you can find another train to join."

Edgar nodded and returned to the Indians. Gertie smiled. She would have plenty of time to talk with him. He would be traveling with the train. She watched as the Indians surrounded him, and they rode south. After they were out of sight, when only a cloud of dust betrayed their direction, she walked back to the camp.

"What was that all about," Abram asked of her. A wrangler was helping him yoke the oxen to the wagon. Gertie quickly tried to make herself useful as the family broke camp.

"There were some Indians blocking the trail. They're angry we chased away the deer. But Mr. Millar spoke with them and he agreed to go with them to hunt somewhere else. I would think this was to console them about any hunting that was interrupted here by our passage. He just left and rode off with them." Gertie paused to add emphasis to her next words. "Mr. Hatch hired him as a scout, so Mr. Millar will be staying with us after all."

Gertie disassembled her makeshift tent. After folding and stowing away the canvas, she made herself busy with the daily chores. Grabbing a bucket she milked one of the communal cows. The cow was docile which thankfully made the task easier because there was no stool upon which to sit. The balancing act included placing her head against the side of the calm beast and reaching under to the udder which was full and ready to be expressed. Upon completion she stood and walked to the wagon where she searched for the crockery churn. Using a piece of loose woven cloth, she strained any debris which had managed to fall into the bucket as she poured the milk. When filled, the churn was stowed on a hook hanging from the side of the wagon. The rocking motion of the wagon would churn the milk into butter by the end of the day.

From his position at the head of the train, Hatch sounded the "Wagons-ho," command. Abram and the other men began snapping their whips against the back of the oxen, and Gertie was once again heading west.

Gertie walked alongside the wagon, as did most of her fellow pioneers. In addition to lightening the load, they had all learned that walking was more comfortable than the hours seated on bone jarring wagons with no springs. The motion which churned butter made for a painful form of transport. She was aware of the burden her presence created for the Smoot family. They had only enough food to feed themselves. As a widowed woman, she was certain they would not let her starve. However, she was uncertain what sacrifices would have to be made to perform this kindness. She spent the day doing her best to be a contributing member of the family as she helped Martha with the wagon and the two children. Briefly, she imagined herself to be Mr. Smoot's second wife.

After lunch, Gertie continually scanned the hillsides for Edgar. She could not keep the tall, lean man from her thoughts. The image of his thick wavy brown hair, soft blue eyes, and stern chiseled chin floated in her mind. She hugged herself, remembering how he had held her in the saddle. She remembered his musky masculine scent and gentle, soothing words as she had cried into his chest.

Edgar had still not returned when the wagons stopped for the night and Gertie became worried. She wondered if the Indians were more dangerous than expected.

"Mr. Hatch," she sought out the wagon master, "has there been any word from Mr. Millar? Could the Indians have turned against him?"

"There has been no sign of him, Mrs. Berg." Seeing the concern in her face, he added, "I'm sorry, but I've no means to search for him. Rest assured, if he is as capable of a scout as he claims to be, he will find his way back to us." He did not address her concern for his safety from Indian retribution.

An hour later, she saw him ride past the camp to Hatch's wagon. He had a deer carcass tied across the back of his horse. She watched as he gave it to Hatch, who in turned invited anyone who wanted some to butcher off a piece of the meat. With the horse's reins in hand, he sauntered back to the Smoot wagon. He handed Martha a slab of the venison.

"Mr. Millar, I am so very glad to see you again." Gertie smiled and waved, as she approached. She pushed her blond, tousled hair back from her face and wished she had found an opportunity for a bath.

Edgar tipped his hat and returned her smile, but said nothing as he unsaddled his horse. He released it to graze with the other livestock.

Speaking to Abram, Edgar said, "Sir, I've no wish to be an inconvenience, but I would appreciate it if you would allow me to camp with you again tonight."

"Of course, Mr. Millar. I hear that you will be traveling with us after all. You are welcome to camp with us as long as you like."

"Thank you, sir. Mr. Hatch has invited me to sup with the wranglers." He turned to Gertie. "Ma'am, are you doing all right?"

"Yes, Mr. Millar, I'm doing very well. I am glad to have another opportunity to speak with you. I fear I was insufficiently grateful to you for saving my life. Yesterday, I-I was still so troubled in my mind to speak clearly. However, I do want to sincerely thank you for your assistance. Without your help, I would surely have perished." She was nearly overtaken by an urge to hug and kiss him.

"I'm obliged to be of service to you, ma'am." He smiled and tipped his hat again before sauntering away.

After supper, Edgar returned and the family gathered around the campfire. Abram bent to push the remaining coal of the fire closer together. When he straightened, he asked, "Tell us, Mr. Millar, what happened today, with the Indians?"

"We stalked some deer along a creek shortly after my departure. I shot two of them; kept the one and gave the other to the Indians. We spent the day hunting buffalo. Their thirty-two caliber Kentucky rifles are insufficient to kill the big beasts. They usually chase them, riding along side stabbing the animals with the spears. One fella was good enough with bow and arrow to hit one several times, but for the most part, they simply run the Buffalo to exhaustion and then pounce on it. However, I was able to bring one down with my Hawken. I gave the meat to them and I spent some time in their village. The Pawnee are an interesting set of redskins. They don't live in teepees and drift across the plains like most other Indians. They have buildings fashioned from straw and mud, and they do some farming.

"Mostly they were very curious about the settlers passing through. They are concerned that the number increases each year, and they are genuinely irritated that the game has been chased away. I told Mr. Hatch that they warned me about the Cheyenne tribe. We will be entering their territory soon, and they are openly angry with the settlers. I suggested he prepare some gifts to give them."

"Gifts? What sort of gifts?" Gertie asked.

"The Indians are just as happy with trinkets as with items of value. In general, they appreciate gifts and consider such a sign of respect for them. They will be less likely to turn violent after being presented with even simple tokens. For example, Mrs. Berg, I gave the Indian who rescued you a small, steel knife as a token of our appreciation."

"Thank you, Mr. Millar; I'm glad you did that. I saw him today... with the other Indians."

"Yes, he was there. He had told them all about our encounter. I expect this is what truly precipitated this morning's visit. Like I said, they are curious about us."

Edgar silently stared into the dying fire for a few minutes as if in contemplation. Turning to address Gertie, he said, "Mrs. Berg, would you care to visit them, see the Indian village? They have heard your story. The chief and his braves were very interested in the adventure of a white woman. They have invited you."

"Indeed, Mr. Millar, I would like to do that."

* * *

Pawnee Village

The following morning after breakfast, Edgar approached Gertie, leading his horse and Mr. Smoot's smaller calico mare.

"Can you ride?" he asked.

"Of course, I can ride a horse," she snorted indignantly.

"Forgive me, I intended no disrespect, ma'am. I only meant like that," he pointed to her skirt. "Can you ride like that?"

"I see. Yes, it will be no trouble." But Gertie knew it would be a challenge. To stay astride in a saddle with a skirt meant some length of leg might be exposed. She did not have any stockings. However, the sense of adventure had been ignited. Determined to visit the village, she accepted Edgar's assistance and mounted the mare.

Edgar's hand tarried a moment longer than necessary as he steadied her calf while she placed her foot securely into the stirrup. Her white flesh had escaped the twisted folds of her skirt to present an ivory temptation in its smoothness. Avoiding the disapproving eyes of the Mormons, she tugged on her skirt to cover what she could.

Mounting his own stallion, he called to her, "This way," and led her to the southeast to begin the trip to the Pawnee Village. They trotted over the hills, taking care not to allow their mounts to misstep on the uneven terrain. Soon, they were out of sight of the wagon train. He slowed his horse to a walk and Gertie rode beside him.

An hour into their adventure, Edgar and Gertie topped the crest of a low hill to expose a valley filled with buffalo. The huge beasts were so tightly mingled that their dark hides obliterated any sight of the greenish-tan grass. They were packed so closely together that the individual animals were indistinguishable within the black morass.

"My word! There must be a thousand of them," Gertie exclaimed. "I've never seen so many. Truly, a magnificent sight."

As they approached the herd, the animals suddenly noticed the invaders. Like a flock of birds taking flight, the entire mass of giant animals rushed away. The thundering roar of thousands of frightened buffalo shook the earth and their hooves trampled all before them as they fled. A gentle breeze blew the cloud of dust which rose from the escaping herd, and all trace of them vanished except for the trampled grasses.

Edgar and Gertie urged their mounts into a walk and rode through the valley as though the beasts had never been there. Gertie had been surprised at the quickness of the buffalo and disappointed at their swift departure. She kept her head high, scanning the empty land for more buffalo as they continued southwest.

"Don't be afraid of these Indians," Edgar said as they drew near to the village. "The Pawnee can get riled up and be as fierce as any Indian, but they are usually kind people. Even if you do become frightened, try not to show it. It is actually insulting to them to display fear."

"Very well, I understand. How much farther is it?"

"Only about another mile."

"Tell me, Mr. Millar, how is it you were traveling with that young Indian?"

"I wasn't traveling with him. I can only surmise he was heading to his hunting place in the early morning, and found you. He must have seen me earlier, and he brought your bonnet to me. And then, he led me to you."

"Why are you traveling alone? With no wagon?"

Edgar chuckled. "Well, the short of it is, I am running away from home. You see, I left my family in Pittsburg two years ago. My father made some bad investments and lost his money. He wanted me to marry a rich widow to secure the family fortune. I refused." He shrugged.

Gertie laughed.

"What's so funny?" he asked.

"Well, Mr. Millar, in some respects, we are the same. I had been unable to find a man I wanted to marry, and my father grew weary of supporting me. He forced me to marry Peter. I only met him a few days before we were married. He was a widower and already had plans to move to Oregon. So, in marrying him, I too set out on this adventure. Now, it seems life's events are carrying me along without my consent." She sighed. "I'm sorry. I don't mean to sound so bitter about it."

"But, you are bitter."

"Well, yes. At least I was more so at first. Women do not have the luxury of running away from these things."

"Yes, I see. Did you love him?"

Gertie scowled at his intrusive question. Softening her face, she said, "No, I didn't. However, Peter was very fair with me."

Edgar looked away, but she saw a glimmer of a smile appear on his lips.

"After I left home," he continued, "I worked on river boats for a while and ended up in the Northwest Wilderness along the Canadian border—a place called Fort Union. That's where I got to know the Indians."

Gertie watched the pain in his expression as he told her the story of how his partner, Bart Adams, had been murdered, and how he had escaped the same fate. The telling of his story heightened her curiosity and interest in the man. Edgar Millar was such a different man than Peter Berg.

"Anyway," he forced a smile, "the fur trade has played out, and it is darn cold up there." His expression brightened, and he chuckled. "So, I decided to head to California."

"Why are you going to California and not Oregon?"

"There was a gold strike there." He motioned for them to stop their horses. He unfolded a newspaper clipping from his pocket and handed it to her. "I read this on the steamboat from Fort Union. I don't think this is widely known yet. The news is slowly working its way east."

She read:

THE CALIFORNIAN

San Francisco, March 15, 1848

Gold Mine Found — In the newly made raceway of the Saw Mill recently erected by Captain Sutter, on the American Fork, gold has been found in considerable quantities. One person brought thirty dollars worth to New Helvetia, gathered there in a short time. California, no doubt, is rich in mineral wealth; great chances here for scientific capitalist. Gold has been found in almost every part of the country.

"My word!"

Astonished, she handed the clipping back to Edgar, and he returned it to his pocket. Nudging his horse with his spurs, he resumed their travel. Gertie's horse followed without her needing to urge it forward with the worn heel of her boot.

"Aye, with the end of the war with Mexico, California is now a United States territory. In a strange coincidence with our current position, the place is mostly populated with Mormons and they found the gold. I dare say it won't be long before the place is overrun with prospectors. I'll be there waiting for them."

"Are you going to prospect for gold?"

He chuckled again. "Oh no, Mrs. Berg, I am not so foolish. A great many men will pan and mine for gold. Many will make money and a few will doubtlessly get rich. It will be the ruin for most of them. I, however, intend to be the merchant who sells food and supplies to these men. The gold they mine will soon be in my hands." He turned to her and smiled. "Well, enough of it to make a good living. That's all I want."

When they topped a hill, she saw the Indian village nestled along the opposite hillside. It was a collection of mud-thatch huts built into the side of the hill in a semi-circle around a spring-fed pond. The pond emptied into a stream and small gardens dotted the sides of the babbling brook.

Edgar halted their approach and waited for the Indians to notice them. One Indian mounted a pony and rode up to them. Gertie recognized him to be the same young man who had helped Edgar rescue her. He spoke a string of words and gestured for them to follow him.

"What did he say?" she asked.

"I've no idea, but I presume he is inviting us to join him," Edgar answered.

In the minute it took for them to reach the village, a throng of men, women, and children formed. Gertie struggled to withhold the apprehension she felt from her face. She had heard so many stories of Indian attacks. Edgar cheerfully waved and she followed suit.

Edgar spoke a long string of unintelligible words when an older man appeared. The Indian's thin gray hair appeared to be at war with the rest of his head. He wore a long feather sticking up behind his head and a leather cape decorated with beads applied with a fine hand-worked skill. He responded to Edgar and the crowd backed away.

"This man is Wasicong, an elder of the tribe. I don't think he is a chief, just a respected wise man. He is the only one who speaks Lakota, which is pretty much the only Indian language I speak. Anyway, he has invited us to join him for a meal."

The two dismounted and Edgar allowed two Indian boys to lead their horses away.

"You're not worried they will steal from us?" Gertie asked as they followed the old man.

He shrugged. "Yes, some concerned, but I accepted that risk when I decided to invite you here."

However, he had not warned her about the risk. She held his arm tightly as they walked. She felt his revolver bump against her hip. An old woman, Gertie presumed her to be the old man's wife, prepared thatch pallets for them in front of their small house. Gertie was curious about what the inside looked like, but did not approach the doorway.

In a disorganized fashion, many of the Indians approached and chatted long strings of unintelligible words. There were several children who had climbed atop the earthen hut dwellings for a better view of the white visitors.

"I can't understand exactly what they are saying," Edgar said. "But they are introducing themselves and welcoming us." Edgar smiled and nodded, and Gertie copied him.

The Indian who had saved her brought a squaw and two toddler children to meet her.

"His name is Anpao," Edgar said.

Gertie repeated the name. She smiled and nodded to his wife and children, but did not attempt to repeat their names as Anpao introduced them.

The women also wore layers of patchwork leather skins. They had leggings which covered their calves, and their fashion of the loincloth was longer, down to their knees. However, it was still open along the sides, exposing their bare thighs and hips in a manner that would have been scandalous in Cincinnati. They also wore a short cape which covered most of their upper body and they carried a large blanket-sized hide that they kept wrapped around their shoulders. This tied under their chins, but they held it closed with their hands whenever they weren't carrying anything.

The young children wore nothing except the short loincloths. Gertie could not distinguish between the boys and girls. The older children wore smaller versions of the adult clothing.

Some of the women began to beat drums and shake tambourines. These instruments had bits of bone tied along thin strips of leather to rattle and slap the taunt, thin membrane. The men danced one at a time. They each strove to outperform the others. At times, they appeared to be aggressive and agitated, which caused Gertie to become nervous. She gripped Edgar's arm.

"I don't think there is a reason to be concerned," he said. "In my experience, most any Indian will be friendly and even helpful by themselves. But when they are in a group, they are driven to demonstrate their courage and manhood. Each one trying to outdo the others can make them aggressive. Most any spark will turn them to violence." He chuckled. "However, if my grasp of the language and actions is right, these young men have only the women on their minds."

Gertie relaxed and walked a few feet away to sit beside several young women in a semicircular line. They were cheering the dancers and Gertie copied them, clapping.

"You shouldn't do that," Edgar said and pushed her hands down. "This is a mating dance of sorts. The men are unmarried and trying to attract wives. By cheering, you are signifying that you are unmarried and seeking a husband."

"Oh." Gertie continued to watch the dancers and smile, but she kept her hands folded in her lap.

The older men approached and sat on the ground. They invited Edgar to join them. Gertie had gotten up to follow him and also sat down. The Indians smoked a communal pipe which they passed from one to the other, and to Edgar. Gertie was not offered the pipe.

One man appeared with his face streaked with red and black paint. Squatting before them, he released a string of angry words and shook his fist. Gertie gripped Edgar's arm in fright.

"Don't be afraid." He put his arm around her and held her tightly while he continued to smile and chat merrily with the angry Indian. Gertie was afraid and struggled to smile. When the Indian began to dance backward she laughed at his comical performance.

"Don't laugh," Edgar cautioned. "He is a Contrarian. He was born backwards, you know—feet first. So he does everything backwards. He is painted for war when he really means to welcome us. He talks angry when he is happy and dances backwards. I don't fully understand the custom, but it is common among the Indians. While he is something of a ceremonial court jester, and he is intended to be funny, you are not supposed to laugh. You are supposed to pretend he is behaving normally."

"He does this all the time?" she asked.

"No, only for ceremonies."

When the Contrarian finished his dance, he walked backward to Gertie. He shook his finger in her face and shouted a string of words.

Edgar exchanged words with the old Indian, Wasicong, and he translated. "The Contrarian says, you are so ugly that the sun must hide when you appear. Which, of course, means you are beautiful and the sun shares your radiance."

Gertie beamed. "Thank you, you are a very handsome man." She nodded to him. Edgar translated to Wasicong and he translated for the Contrarian. He, in turn, scowled and stomped away backwards.

When the dancing completed, a woman knelt before Gertie and tugged on her shoe.

"I gather that she has never seen a lace-up type shoe before," Edgar opined.

Gertie took off her shoe and handed it to the woman. Surprisingly the woman ignored it and held Gertie's foot. Gertie resisted the urge to pull her foot away. The woman laid her palm along the underside of Gertie's foot. She examined Gertie's calf and ran her finger along the multitude of scratches Gertie had gotten while walking so many miles through the brush. Gertie giggled, trying to hold still during the ticklish maneuver. The woman said something and ran away.

"What was that about?" Gertie asked as she put her shoe back on.

"I don't know," Edgar answered.

Clay bowls with roasted meat and vegetables were passed around. Gertie found the contents delicious and she ate heartily of venison, corn, onions, and carrots. She had not eaten a better meal in a long time. She emptied her bowl and smiled with satisfaction.

"We should be heading back," Edgar said when they had finished the meal. "I'll make our excuses to our host."

While Edgar conversed with the older Indian, the woman who had examined Gertie's foot returned. She handed Gertie a pair of moccasin boots. They had high tops to protect her calves, and had been worked using the same skill she had noticed on the elder's buckskin. They were embroidered and decorated with fringe and beads.

"My goodness, they're beautiful. That's what she was doing; she was measuring my foot." Gertie took off her shoes and put on the moccasins. Holding her skirt up, she danced a jig while laughing. "Please thank her for me." Edgar conversed with Wasicong who translated. "I don't have anything to give her in return," Gertie continued.

"It's not necessary. I believe she is Anpao's mother, and she is responding to the knife I gave him."

"Oh, please thank her again." Gertie hugged the woman.

Edgar engaged in a long, complex conversation with the Indians while the boys returned with their horses. Wearing her new moccasins, Gertie mounted her horse. Edgar put her shoes into his saddle bag and swung astride his stallion.

"What was that all about?" she asked.

"They were warning me again that the Cheyenne are angry with the settlers. He says we should use haste as we travel through their lands." He turned away and urged his horse up the hill. "And they were congratulating me."

"Why? What for?"

"It seems they think you are my wife."

Gertie laughed, but a new vision of Edgar holding her tightly in his arms, kissing her hungrily, entered her mind.

Waving goodbye, the two companions urged their horses into a trot to hurry back to the wagons. Arriving at dusk, Gertie sat by the Smoot family campfire and related her Pawnee adventure to both the adults and children. Others in the wagon train came close to hear her tale. Everyone admired her new moccasins and the skill employed in their creation. Gertie spoke of the kindness of the Pawnee and told the children about the "backwards Indian." They laughed in disbelief of such an individual.

After the children were put to bed, Mr. Hatch called for a meeting.

"I'm sure you have all heard of yesterday's incident with the Indians. And I am sure you have all heard exaggerated reports of Indian violence. However, I want to assure you that this train is in no danger. The Pawnee have never been known to hurt anyone. Mr. Millar has spent the day with these Indians and he assures me that they are only interested in our haste to depart their favorite hunting grounds along the river.

"Yet, there is the matter of the Cheyenne tribes ahead of us. These Indians are known to be more aggressive. Yet, we have little to fear as we are such a large train with many armed men. The natives are known to harass small groups of settlers that they can easily intimidate and overpower. There have been no reports of attacks upon trains as large as ours.

"As wise men, though, we will be taking additional precautions. We will be traveling with the wagons closer together and with our children and livestock between the two parallel rows. Everyone is urged to keep together and cooperate with my men as they guide you.

"Now, most importantly, when we camp, everyone must stay close. No one is to wander away from the protection of the sentries. While I don't expect it, the Indians have been known to assault individuals who are out of sight of the camp. Mr. Stoddard, I believe, has a personal experience to relate." Hatch gestured to the man standing beside him.

"Yes," Mr. Stoddard began, "it was last year when my brother and his family made this journey. From Fort John, he sent me this letter." He held up the paper. "It relates an experience where his wife was gathering flowers. While she was within sight of their wagons, she was at some distance away. Two Indians approached their wagons and through hand signals asked for food. Not wishing to anger them, my brother gave them what was left of a deer they had killed the previous day. The Indians took it. And then, as they rode away, they took the woman too.

"My brother and his eldest son gathered and saddled their horses to give chase, but the Indians were hard to track. At dusk they found the Indians, who shot arrows into my nephew, killing him. With the rapid discharge of his revolver, my brother was able to scatter the Indians and recover his wife." Mr. Stoddard's voice trembled as he finished. "She had been divested of all clothing and other insults upon her were unspeakable."

He looked down and Hatch gave his shoulder a comforting squeeze.

"From this account," Hatch continued, "I want you all to understand that in keeping yourself safe, you also keep your family safe. Mr. Stoddard's brother lost his son in the rescue of his wife. Therefore, keep yourselves safe and keep your children close." Hatch let these words sink into their memories. "One last thing, Mrs. Hatch will no longer ride ahead to select a location for our midday meal. In order to get through the Cheyenne territory faster, we will be driving fourteen hour days. Because of the burden to the oxen we will be stopping for only a bit longer than normal for a rest at noon. As you are tending your stock and feeding your families, take special care to keep an eye out for Indians." He swallowed. "That's all."

CHAPTER EIGHT

June 17, 1848
Cheyenne Territory

Much of the joyful camaraderie among the settlers was gone in the morning. For the next several days, everyone worried about the Indians, and kept their attention on the business of survival. Each morning, Mr. Millar and the other scout rode ahead, searching for signs of the Cheyenne. Daily they returned with deer or buffalo meat to supplement the group's food supply. At the end of continuously exhausting days, everyone took to their beds with little conversation.

On the third day, they reached the Platte River and camped in an area where the river bank broadened into a mile wide, marshy plain. The ground was too soggy to support fully grown cottonwood trees so the sparse brush was a combination of willow and stunted cottonwood.

"Mr. Millar, are those Indians?" Gertie pointed to a row of campfires on the north side of the river.

"No, those are campsites of other pioneers along the north bank of the river."

"Where did they come from?"

"They came across the Missouri River north of Independence—in Iowa. There is a new steam-powered ferry there, and it shortens the trip. They have been following the Platte." He pointed to the west. "The river splits ahead. We will soon cross the South Platte River, and those people will be crossing the North Platte River when we reach Fort John. Then we will all head out into the desert."

She watched the distant campfires, mesmerized as she pondered the families engaged in their evening's activities.

The following morning, the Hatch wagon train continued due west, while the river angled to the northwest, thus they separated from the river in search of firm, dry land which would support their wagons. Two days later, they reached the South Platte River.

"You can't see it from here," Edgar told Gertie, "but the North Platte is a few miles north. We'll cross the South Platte tomorrow morning, and then we will follow the North Platte." The river valley was so broad Gertie could not see the ridge of hills which formed the valley's northern boundary. However, Edgar pointed toward a line of hills from the west that split the valley in two. "The North Platte continues along the other side of those hills."

As Gertie and Martha were cleaning the dishes from their supper, it began to rain a slow, steady drizzle. Mr. Smoot hastened to erect a canvas awning beside the wagon and the two women dashed for its cover.

"At least it will keep the little buggers away," Martha remarked.

Gertie agreed that the one benefit of the rain was that it spared them from the torturous onslaught of mosquitoes; only a few found them beneath the canvas. That night the rain came down in buckets and drenched the canvas on the wagons and the travelers.

"The rain has soaked the ground, making a river crossing too risky," Mr. Hatch announced the following morning. A respite from travel was declared and most families used the time to make repairs and wash their clothes in the river. In this soaked area, there were no trees or brush of any kind which meant there was no privacy. To allow the women to bathe, vertical walls were constructed on the riverbank by stretching canvas sheet between tall stakes in the ground. It was in this provided seclusion where the women stripped to their under garments and bathed. One or two of the younger women were brave enough to disrobe totally and submerge themselves in the cooling, soothing waters. At a safe distance away and out of sight, the children and some of the men waded in the water and washed fully clothed. The heat of the day soon dried their garments. Nervous, Mr. Hatch ordered the wranglers to keep a close watch on the hillsides for Indians. At this point, even though it was to be almost a holiday from travel, everyone was cautious. The men were vigilant as they climbed from the river in dripping shirts and pants. The children were not so vigilant and played and laughed as they enjoyed the day of no travel.

Edgar did not stay in camp. He crossed the river on his horse early in the morning and scouted the far bank for firm land which would support the weight of the wagons. The search had not been an easy crossing. Wet soggy ground was also dangerous for a horse and rider. Edgar had intently looked all around and downward to make sure his chocolate stallion did not become dangerously ensnared by the swampy earth. A broken leg or even a pulled tendon would have been a tragedy. As he scouted for solid earth, he found an area with some underlying rock which made for a firmer roadway for the wagon train. He had brought wooden stakes with him to mark the chosen route. Edgar returned to Mr. Hatch and pointed out the pathway for the travelers. It was the safest possible crossing under the circumstances.

The wagon train lost no time as they began the crossing of the river the following morning. The river was two-thirds of a mile wide. Most of the riverbed was firm sand and the water less than two feet deep, but several hidden holes were filled with quicksand. To safeguard their crossing, ropes were used to bind each wagon to the one before it. Thus, when a wagon sank into the soft sand, those in front of it would help pull it free. The wranglers used their horses to pull the lead wagon through the deep spots.

Gertie was fearful of entering the slow moving brown water. Memories of the tragic river crossing weeks before swam through her mind. She sat in the wagon, atop their supplies, with the two children. She was uncertain if she was reassuring them or if they were comforting her. They watched Mr. Smoot as he urged the oxen into the water. Edgar was astride his horse beside them. Although the first several minutes of the crossing were uneventful, she wished she had chosen to ride with him where she would have felt safer.

She shrieked when the wagon dropped several inches with a sudden jolt. A few feet further along it sprang up again as the wheels climbed out of the quicksand pit. This up and down pattern continued shaking the life out of those in the wagon. The children cried, the women screamed, and the men swore. At one point, the wagon sank so deep that it began to float. As planned, the ropes attached to the wagon in front pulled tight and eased them across the deep hole. While some water leaked through the wagon's wooden planks, it drained away as soon as they were back on firm sand.

Once on the opposite bank, they followed the stakes left by Edgar which led north to the hill. The hill rose sharply, too steep for the wagons to proceed along the direct path. To avoid the difficult climb, they turned east, around the hill before resuming their westward trek. The wagons moved along canted on the hillside at an uncomfortable angle, but the ground was firm and they could continue their bouncing transport around the foot of the hill.

That evening, the weary travelers camped beside a stream between the hills and the North Platte River. The firmer soil supported a few cottonwood trees and thick brush along the banks of the stream. Gertie, Martha, and another woman, Mrs. Ester Coombs, went into the brush to use the latrine.

"Look, sand cherries." Ester picked a small fruit from a bush and ate it. "They're ripe. We can make some pies."

The three women began picking the small, dark red fruits. They collected slightly more than they ate as they followed the row of bushes. After half an hour, Gertie looked around. Disoriented, she could not see the campsite through the brush.

"Where are we?" she asked. "Shouldn't we be getting back to camp?"

"Oh, we are not far, see the hills?" Martha pointed toward the southern hills. "We will be back before anyone misses us."

"What are you women doing?" Rees's harsh voice startled Gertie. Turning around, she watched Rees and Edgar ride their horses toward them. "Everyone is looking for you. Why did you wander off?" He continued, with an angry snarl.

"We-we were picking sand cherries for pies," Ester said, as though this would be sufficient justification.

The men dismounted.

"Why don't you see these two women back to their husbands," Edgar said to Rees. "I'll take care of Mrs. Berg."

Mr. Rees used his knife to chop a branch from a bush. He stripped it of leaves to create a two-foot long rod the diameter of a finger. He made a practice slap against his boot and the women jumped with the sharp report.

He means to use a switch on me, the startled Gertie's thoughts illuminated.

"See that you do... take care of her," Rees said, with impatience. He and handed the rod to Edgar.

As though he was herding calves, Rees urged Martha and Ester back to camp.

Edgar approached Gertie. "Don't you remember the rules?" he asked, but answered his own question. "You are to remain within sight of camp."

Gertie scanned the brush, looking for some evidence that she could still see the camp, but she could not. Her belly quivered as she recalled how Peter would 'take care' of her. However, the switch had a far more menacing look to it than anything Peter had produced.

"I'm sorry. I guess we simply got carried away, picking the fruits. We're not in any danger."

"How do you know? We rode upon you unseen. And we weren't even trying to sneak up on you. A dozen Indians could be hiding in this brush."

"As I said, we made a mistake. I'm sorry."

"I'm sorry too, but you see, we can't possibly just let this go. Something must be done to ensure this doesn't happen again." He locked eyes with her.

Her gut clenched and her voice froze in her throat. She could only nod.

"I am responsible for you." His voice was in a smooth, even tone.

Gertie's spine shivered as she stared at the switch in his hand.

She thought of running, but her feet remained rooted. She opened her lips and tried to suck in a breath, but her diaphragm froze. She tried to convince herself he was not really angry.

"I'm willing to settle for your solemn promise to never place yourself in danger again. I'm sure you understand what the Mormons have planned for the other women." He held up the rod.

Gertie imagined the abuse her friends must be enduring at that very moment.

"Sir, let me say again how sorry I am," she whispered. "And I assure you, this will *never* happen again."

"The Indians are not a civilization as you might imagine. While much is made of their violence, they are not naturally violent. They would rather humiliate their enemies than kill them. Don't misunderstand me; they can easily be provoked into murderous ways. Horses are their symbol of wealth and currency. Instead of murdering a foe, they seek to steal his horses. Additionally, they view women as property and practice slavery. They humiliate their enemies by stealing their women and children. Make no mistake; an Indian angry with our passage through their lands would delight in kidnapping you. And, it would be impossible to rescue you."

Suddenly dizzy, she braced a hand against a piece of driftwood.

"Are you all right?" he asked.

Edgar sat on a narrow stump of a collapsed cottonwood tree and eased her down on his lap.

"I'm so sorry for endangering myself and the others," she said.

He is saving me again.

The sense of safety filled her as she cuddled in his arms.

"Thank you," she whispered. Realizing she had been crying, she stopped the quiet sobs.

"For not beating you?"

"Yes, and for caring so much about my safety."

"Indeed, I do care for your safety and I may not be so lenient in the future. So, you had best pay close attention to the rules from now on." Again, he held up the rod.

She nodded while holding her face nestled against his chest.

Edgar hugged her again. His finger lifted her chin. In the most surprising manner, he gently kissed her. Momentarily startled, Gertie trembled before melting into his arms.

"We'd better be getting back," he whispered as their lips parted. He helped her to her feet. "You had better do a good job of pretending that I switched you. And, don't forget the sand cherries. I am looking forward to a pie." He grinned, and for a moment, they laughed.

Edgar tucked the rod into his gun belt. Leading his horse, they walked back to camp.

Martha and Ester were both standing before Mr. Hatch. He was lecturing them while they rubbed the backsides of their skirts. Without being told, Gertie took her place beside them. Struggling to keep a straight face, she dabbed away fake tears with one hand while rubbing her bottom with the other.

"Well, Mrs. Berg, as I was telling these two women, should such an event occur again, it will be the men who risk their lives in search of you that will administer the punishment. Do you understand me?"

"Yes, sir," the three women responded.

"Now, we are all expecting some cherry pie, so get busy."

They hastily prepared the pies and baked them in large Dutch ovens suspended over the fires.

After serving the perfectly browned and mouth watering pies, Gertie retired to her makeshift tent under the Smoot's wagon.

Pulling the blanket around her shoulders, she attempted to reconcile the deep heat which had formed between her thighs. Exhausted as she was, she could not get Edgar out of her mind. His proclamation that he would 'take care' of her had clearly implied more than merely switching her bottom. His warm embrace as he held her had been so much more comforting than any embrace from Peter. And then, there was his kiss. Her belly quivered whenever she thought about his lips tenderly touching hers. She allowed the image of Edgar's fingers touching her to fill her mind.

A crescendo of distant thunder distracted her from her thoughts. She had experienced the plain's ferocious thunderstorms already. The canvas forming the sides of her little tent was not anchored to the ground and it had done little to keep out the rain when the wind blew. She eased open the canvas flap to watch the jagged, brilliant lightning on the horizon and wondered if the rain was coming her way.

In the dying embers of the campfire, she watched Edgar prepare for the storm. He spread his buffalo hide out flat and staked the four hairy stubs of hide where the great plains beast's legs had once been. With a stick about as long as his arm, he propped up the front of the fur covered skin and created a small tent. Into the tent, he placed an oiled canvas to keep the ground water from seeping upward. Edgar crawled inside. The hide would be impervious to rain. Although it would get heavy as it soaked up the water, he would stay dry.

A sudden, closer crash of lightning startled her, and before she was aware of what she was doing, she dashed outside her tent. Running through the early drops of rain, she crawled into the small tent beside Edgar.

In a subsequent flash of lightning, she watched the surprise on his face.

"I'm sorry, the lightning scared me. I'll go back." Gertie started to crawl out from under the buffalo hide, but his warm hand stopped her.

"No, you can stay, Mrs. Berg. I know your tent does not do well in the storms."

"Thank you, Mr. Millar." She nervously ran her tongue across her lips. "But I-I would rather that you call me Gertie," she stammered.

"Mm, you should call me Edgar." His voice was slow and confident.

She swallowed the lump which had just formed in her throat and tried to decide exactly what her intentions were. The memory of his kiss still burned upon her lips. Peter's lovemaking had been enjoyable, but she yearned for Edgar. She felt vulnerable, but was ready for him to take her.

He rolled onto his side and cradled her face in his palms. He pulled their faces together. She closed her eyes and parted her lips. Her tongue touched his as they kissed. She inhaled his aroma and pressed her lips tightly against his mouth. Slowly, he pulled away.

"What is it you want from me?" he asked.

Her belly clenched with the sound of his words, but she could not force words of her own to form. When she said nothing, he released her.

Why does he not take me now?

Gertie could not reconcile her emotions with what she knew to be decent common sense. She wanted him to make love with her, but she knew this would be completely inappropriate. It was totally improper for her to even be in the bed beside him. She wanted him, but she could not say the words.

He's being such a gentleman.

A flash of lightning revealed his face with his eyes watching her. Edgar remained silent as he removed his hands from her face. After several heartbeats of quiet there was another flash of light from the storm. In the brief moment of illumination, Gertie saw that his eyes were closed. She watched as he quietly continued to sleep. Obviously tired but relaxed as he rested beside her. This realization soothed her need and she enjoyed his closeness. In his slumber, she felt his body shift; his hip pressed against hers. She rolled to her side and pressed her back to him. The rhythmic warmth of his breath caressed her neck. Feeling safe with him, she drifted to sleep.

CHAPTER NINE

June 21, 1848
Company

In the predawn hour, Edgar nudged Gertie.

"What is it?" she asked.

"It's time for me to go to work." However, he didn't move. They stared at each other in the darkness. Embarrassed, Gertie wondered what they should do, waking up together. Hesitantly, he kissed her and crawled out from under the buffalo hide tent. He glanced around; seeing no one he gestured to her. "You should go too."

Bundling her underskirt about her thighs, Gertie scampered to her own tent.

"Goodbye," she whispered as she closed the canvas flap. "Don't worry with the bedding, I will dry and pack your things."

Gertie, waited and listened to the familiar sounds as he strapped on his revolver and picked up the saddle. After his footfalls drifted into silence, she dressed in her blouse and skirt. She couldn't stop thinking of Edgar. His familiar sounds and the recollection of the smell of his body fogged her brain and made it hard to concentrate. Ready for the day, she reemerged from under the wagon and lit the campfire.

Oh, what I wouldn't give for a cup of coffee.

As the cooking pans warmed, she watched a wrangler help Edgar catch his horse. Saddling the stallion, he mounted and joined the other scout. Together, they rode west. She rolled his buffalo hide and disassembled her tent, and waited for the Smoot family to arise.

While still in the Cheyenne Indian territory, the wagons maintained a progression which kept them close together. Fearful her face would mirror her secret thoughts of Edgar, Gertie was reluctant to ride in the wagon with Martha.

"I wish to stretch my legs," she told Mr. Smoot.

This was the truth. She still felt pangs in her legs from the twisted position in which she had slept under the buffalo hide.

Two hours into the day, as the wagons steadily rolled along the trail, Edgar galloped back to the wagons. Gertie watched as he frantically spoke with Mr. Hatch. Mr. Rees joined their conversation. Moments later, Hatch gathered two of the wranglers, and the three men followed Edgar at a gallop.

Rees hastily rode along the two parallel rows of wagon. "Prepare for Indian attack. Men take your rifles in hand. Women and children into the wagons. Keep your teams moving and stay close together." Rees continued down the line stopping to repeat the message.

Abram took Martha's place on the wagon seat. Gertie gathered the two children and hoisted them into the wagon. She jumped up behind them.

"Here," Martha handed her the gunpowder and shot, "after Abram fires, he will hand the rifle to you. I'll hand him a fresh rifle while you are to swab out the recently fired one. Then, I'll reload it."

The two women crouched atop the pile of supplies, covering the children with their bodies. Gertie could see nothing outside the wagon. Abram fiercely whipped the oxen to urge them along faster. At noontime, they paused long enough to water the beasts. Martha passed around some dried meat, but no one got out of the wagon. An hour later, they came to a halt. Pushing the canvas covering aside, Gertie observed four new wagons beside the train. A group of women were sitting on the ground, crying beside three graves.

"Oh, my God, what has happened?" she exclaimed.

"Wait here and water the oxen," Abram commanded. He walked to a gathering of men who stood off a distance from the crying women.

Gertie searched for Edgar and found him on horseback along the crest of the hill to the south. He had his rifle in hand and was studying the distant hills, watching for Indians.

Mr. Rees rode along the line telling everyone, "Do what is necessary, but stay near your wagons. We won't be staying here long."

Gertie and Martha took the children to the least exposed side of the wagon so they could relieve themselves. Gertie and Martha also took the opportunity to take advantage of the same privacy to ease their aching bladders. The hours of riding in the rough wagons had jarred them all terribly.

"What has happened?" Martha asked of Abram when they returned.

"Cheyenne attacked them early this morning." He nodded toward the four new wagons. "Their leader, Mr. Clark, and his son were killed along with another man. Mr. Hatch has offered to allow them to continue to Fort John with us. We are going to get moving soon, and keep going until dark."

Worried for Edgar's safety, Gertie turned her gaze to the south. Edgar was riding along the ridge, heading west. His rifle cradled in his arms.

Mr. Hatch assigned two of the oldest boys among the settlers to work the oxen teams for the two widowed women, Mrs. Clark and Mrs. Howe. Soon, they were back on the trail.

The hours passed slowly for Gertie as her bones were once again assaulted by the rough, rocking ride of the wagon. It was dusk when they stopped again. They did not light any fires and ate only dried venison. With the moonlight, the sky was bright enough that people could walk around without falling or bumping into oxen or wagons. After the teams were attended to and the venison eaten, everyone gathered around their new companions.

"Yes, it was positively terrible," Mrs. Clark began telling her story. "I never heard such an uproar before. With a deafening yell, they attacked us from the hillside," she pointed south. "Singing their war songs with their shrill war whoops. It was a sound I shall never forget." She shuddered. "While these Indians drew our attention, others crept out from the trees along the river and stole our horses. When he spotted these vermin, my husband stood to fire his rifle." She paused to wipe her eyes. "That's when he was shot dead. My son was killed too." She hugged her daughter. "Seems they were only interested in the horses. Once they had 'em, they rode away to the south as quickly as they came. Beth's husband," she nodded toward Mrs. Howe, "was shot dead as well."

"Mrs. Berg?" Mr. Hatch pulled Gertie aside.

"Yes?"

"Mrs. Howe is all alone. I was wondering if you might be able to offer some comfort to her tonight."

Gertie approached the grieving woman. "Excuse me, I'm Gertrude Berg. Like you, I lost my husband and I am now traveling alone." Gertie waited until the woman's eyes registered her comprehension. "Would you like some companionship tonight? I could stay with you."

"Why, yes-yes, thank you."

Gertie shared a portion of the dried meat with her. "I'm sorry, but we've been instructed not to light any fires tonight."

"Yes, I know." She accepted the food from Gertie. "Thank you." She tugged off a bite and chewed it. "I see you are not Mormon?"

"No, I was traveling with a different wagon train. My husband and I had turned back, but he was murdered." Gertie paused; she found it difficult to recall Peter's face. "I had known Mrs. Smoot—Martha—while we were camped in Independence. She and her husband invited me to travel with them, but, of course, that was westward."

"I see. My Christian name is Elizabeth, but everyone calls me Beth."

"I'm Gertie." The two women lightly shook hands. "I'm not exactly sure what is to become of me when this train turns southward towards the Great Salt Lake." Gertie's thought turned to Edgar and she hoped their fates would remain entwined. "The Smoots are a wonderful family and their kindness is evident. I'll introduce you to them tomorrow they may be able to advise you or offer you help as they did me."

"I'm not at all sure what is to become of me either. However, there is no choice but to continue west—for now."

Mrs. Clark and her daughter joined them.

"Grace, this is Mrs. Berg. She lost her husband a while back." Beth turned to Gertie. "Mrs. Clark's husband is—was my brother. And this is their daughter, Marjorie."

"It is very nice to meet you, Mrs. Clark," Gertie said. "I'm very sorry about the loss of your husband."

Wiping a tear from her eye, Mrs. Clark said, "Please, call me Grace. We three can travel together, eh, Mrs. Berg? The merry widows," she strained a brief smile but her true emotion was betrayed by a solitary tear which ran down her cheek. "We can help each other."

"Indeed, but you must call me Gertie."

When they finished eating, Grace and Marjorie returned to their wagon. Edgar walked up carrying his bedroll.

"Here you are, Mrs. Berg," he said.

"Mrs. Howe, this is Mr. Millar, the man who rescued me. He has been courteously looking after me along this journey," Gertie introduced Edgar.

"Yes, Mr. Millar and I are acquainted." Beth sniffled and wiped her eyes. "It was he who discovered us and buried my husband." She wondered how many men would be buried along this trail.

Edgar removed his hat. "Ma'am, I was wondering if I might camp beside your wagon tonight?" he asked.

"Certainly, Mr. Millar, you are always welcome here." Beth climbed into her wagon. "Uh, Gertie, would you care to join me? Or, do you have other accommodations?" She glanced toward Edgar and wondered how she could know about her and Edgar.

"Certainly, I will stay with you," Gertie responded, hiding her eyes. "I have been sleeping under Mr. Smoot's wagon. It will be very nice to sleep inside a wagon." She climbed into the wagon. She took one last glance at Edgar before tying the canvas flap closed.

Beth and her husband had fashioned a very comfortable bed in their wagon. They had used boards to construct a shelf atop their supplies and had a real mattress. Gertie experienced her soundest sleep in several weeks. When she awoke, Beth was gone. Climbing out of the wagon in the gray, early light, she found her companion obeying the no-campfire rule and preparing a cold breakfast.

Gertie accepted the cold potatoes and dried meat.

"Mr. Millar left earlier." Beth glanced to see the impact of her next words upon Gertie's face. "He is not Mormon either. Is he *with* you?"

"Uh, yes, to some extent. He has taken responsibility for me. He's not Mormon, but has experience with Indians. Mr. Hatch hired him to help see us through the Indian territory."

"I see," Beth said. "If you have no better situation here, I would like for you to stay with me. I have food and supplies for two people. Of course, Mr. Millar is welcome to camp with us as well."

"Thank you, I am grateful for your offer. I was getting very cramped, sleeping on the ground."

"He is, uh, the same size as my husband." Beth looked away. "I offered my husband's clothes to Mr. Millar and he accepted." She again paused to watch the expression on Gertie's face.

"With the coming hot summer days, I'm sure he will be most grateful to get out of his hot leather Indian clothing." Gertie instantly regretted her phrasing, but she did imagine what Edgar might look like as he undressed—naked. Saying nothing more and trying to hide her smile, she chewed another bite.

Two wranglers arrived and hitched two yoke of oxen. The 'wagons-ho' command passed down the row of wagons. Gertie watched the dust lift as the wagons resumed their travel. The teenager assigned to manage Beth's team snapped his whip on the haunches of the oxen and the wagon lurched forward.

That night Edgar ate with the wranglers before joining them. When Gertie headed to bed, he walked to the back of the wagon with her. In the shadows he pulled her close and tightly hugged her. Quickly, he kissed her. Her core throbbed with the want, the need of him. Parting, Edgar steadied her hand as she climbed into the wagon.

At first Beth didn't say anything as Gertie undressed and lay down beside her. In the dark silence, she whispered, "I heard the other women talking that Mr. Millar beat you. Is it true?"

Gertie sighed. "No. I and two other women broke the rules and endangered the wagon train a few days ago. They were punished by their husbands and Mr. Millar was assigned to do the same for me. But, he only gave me a good tongue lashing, that's all. We pretended he had actually done it."

Beth chuckled.

"It wasn't funny—"

"Yes, I know. I am sorry, but you see you said tongue lashing. That is what my husband used to call it... call it when he—he gave me a tongue lashing between the thighs. When you said the words, it made me imagine Mr. Millar doing such a thing, and I laughed. I'm sorry."

Gertie was silent and Beth mistook her silence for anger.

"I know he's your man," she continued. "I have no designs upon him."

But Gertie had not been angry. She had been shocked into silence with the mental image Beth had given her. She tried to imagine what such a tongue lashing would feel like. When Beth's breathing morphed into soft snores, Gertie eased out of the wagon and crawled under the buffalo hide to be with Edgar. He said nothing as he took her in his arms and kissed her. His presence and the touch of his body made her feel safe and warm.

* * *

Sleepless Night

"You are being very naughty," said Edgar, but he did not kick her out.

Her belly clenched. She was unsure whether he was teasing her, or if he was serious. She knew her behavior was inappropriate and the Mormons would certainly kick them both out of the wagon train if they were caught together.

"I was-was hoping you would deal with my behavior an-another way," she whispered.

He shifted to his side and his hand caressed her cheek. When she didn't resist his advance, he traced his fingers along her jawbone to her neck. He released the top button of her chemise.

"Are you sure about this?" he whispered.

She tried to say 'yes', but the word caught in her throat. She nodded.

The potential threat of getting caught vanished from her consciousness as he rolled her onto her back. Kissing her, he eased his hand under her chemise. He traced his fingers along the soft underside of her breast.

She pulled her lips away from his kiss and gasped for breath. Edgar paused as if questioning her.

"*Yes*, please more." Gertie gasped. She wanted this delight to last forever. He slowed his pace and tenderly they began to make love. Edgar knew all the right things to do.

Although her eyes were closed, sudden star bursts appeared in her eyes. She bit down on the collar of his shirt to stifle her squeals of pleasure. When they were fulfilled and lay quietly, she pressed her face into his chest. Breathless, she panted. Lovemaking had never been like this before.

"Open your eyes and look at me," he softly commanded.

As she complied, a flash of lightning illuminated his face hovering over her. It was rugged and handsome, covered with a sheen of sweat and all she wanted to think about was what they had just done together. So engrossed in the act of love making, Gertie had not been aware of the approaching storm. Edgar got comfortable beside her and drifted off to sleep. She remained awake, not from fear of the thunder and lightning, but to allow herself to continue, with the aid of each splash of storm fire across the sky, to enjoy his sleeping repose.

CHAPTER TEN

June 23, 1848
Chimney Rock

As the wagon train continued westward, the land became barren and dry—nothing but sand and sagebrush. The nearly flat land of the plains gave way to rolling hills. Gertie swore each hill was taller and steeper than the one before. The patches of cottonwood trees were few and far between. The river narrowed and deepened. The swift moving water was now impossible to cross. The game also became scarce. The scouts were lucky to bring home one deer per day. There were occasional, small buffalo herds. The huge shaggy beasts were shot and brought down by the hunters. While unable to move the massive carcasses of the buffalo, they were able to butcher and return with the best of the meat.

A new animal became prevalent. Prairie chickens were frequently seen scurrying around in the sagebrush. While these birds did occasionally fly, they preferred to elude predators by running on the ground. Nonetheless, they provided sport for the teenage boys with shotguns and they provided several tasty meals. This sport was marred by the death of one boy who was accidentally shot and killed. At nine years of age, he had become excited with the hunt of a particularly plump prairie chicken and unknowingly stepped into the line of fire of one of his companions.

As with the other deaths along the Oregon Trail, a time was given for mourning and burial. The parents were inconsolable and it was only with the help of their remaining children that they were able to pull themselves together and continue the journey. Each family among the wagons stopped to give their respects and added their prayers to those of the survivors. As Gertie mourned the sad events of the day, she recalled a woman who had stepped on a rattlesnake and died from its venom.

Accidentally firing guns, rattlesnakes, Indians, there was so much danger on the Oregon Trail.

Edgar and Gertie joined others to express their condolences. After a quiet meal of buffalo steaks, conversation turned to the future.

"Is this the desert?" Gertie asked of Edgar.

"Oh, no, this is a veritable oasis compared with what is to come." Seeing her inquisitive expression, he continued, "I've not been there, mind you, but I have heard from the other scout that a few days after Fort John we leave the Platte River. The area west, for hundreds of miles, is the desert. There are springs, so we will have water available most every day."

Gertie examined the horizon.

"What are you going to do when we get to Fort John? Mr. Hatch said you could only ride with the wagon train that far," she said.

"I'll find a scout job with another train. There are lots of wagon trains passing through Fort John."

Gertie remembered Martha's statement that the Mormon Trail turned south at Fort Bridger, but she had no idea where that was. "Where does the path to California diverge from the Oregon Trail?"

"At Fort Bridger. That is several hundred miles, on the other side of the desert from Fort John."

She sighed. "I wonder what will happen to me. I fear I'm destined to become a Mormon." Gertie had a dream several nights earlier. In the dream she was Abram's second wife and had been pregnant while living with her sister-wife Martha.

"You don't want to stay with the Smoots?"

"I hadn't thought about it too much, but no. I want to continue on to Oregon." She turned to see the impact of her next words. "Or, perhaps I'll go to California."

With you!

She looked into his eyes to see if he caught her true meaning. He turned to meet her gaze and smiled. However, he did not respond. What she really wanted, was for him to make his way to the Great Salt Lake even if he did it with another wagon train. There, she imagined him rescuing her and taking her on to California.

Is this merely a widow's dream?

Gertie, Beth, and Grace became close friends. Distancing herself from the Mormons, Gertie joined the two other widows. While the other families each cooked for themselves, the three widows camped together and cooked one shared meal. Grace was the oldest while Gertie was the youngest; a dozen years separated their ages. Being a mother, Mrs. Howe adopted the role of seniority and mothered the other two. Gertie enjoyed having a sage mother figure to watch over her once again. Edgar continued to eat with Mr. Hatch's men, but he slept beside Beth and Gertie's wagon. Gertie always felt safe with Edgar near the wagon.

The wagon train camped early one day under a tall spire of rock; the most prominent landscape feature she had ever seen.

"This is Chimney Rock. This marks the end of the Indian Territory," Mr. Hatch proclaimed. "We'll camp early and have a celebration."

Herding the livestock around in a circle, the grass and brush were trampled flat to create a dance floor. Men and women brought out their various musical instruments and the impromptu band struck up a lively tune. One man began calling out a barn dance cadence. Gertie danced polkas and quadrilles with several unmarried men, but mostly she danced with Edgar. As darkness settled, the families returned to their wagons. Gertie realized how things could change so quickly on the trail—one minute death and irresolvable grief, the next, the joy of dancing and laughing with fellow revelers well into the night. When the evening came to an end, exhausted, she made her way back to the widows' wagon.

Gertie climbed into the wagon, removed her day clothes, and lay on the bed next to Beth.

"You know," Beth whispered, "you probably want to keep your nocturnal adventures secret from everyone else here, but if you want to be with Mr. Millar, you needn't bother trying to sneak behind my back."

Gertie was stunned into silence with her frank speech.

"Do you love him?" Beth continued.

Gertie swallowed and tried to imagine what the honest answer to the question was. "I don't know for sure. I think so." Gertie was ashamed to admit she didn't know what love truly felt like. Beth didn't respond, and Gertie asked, "Did you love your husband?"

"Of course I did. He was a wonderful man."

Gertie let the silence between them hang for a while. "I didn't love Peter," she confessed. "I barely knew him. My father forced me to marry him." Gertie related her brief courtship and marriage. "Why don't you have children?" she finished.

"I was with child once, but it wasn't meant to be." Beth was quiet for several moments and Gertie thought she heard Beth softly crying. "We-we had decided to wait until we were settled in Oregon to try again."

The two women lay silent for several minutes.

"Go on," Beth nudged her. "You don't have to wait for me to pretend to be asleep anymore." She poked her elbow into Gertie's side again. "However, be careful of the others. If you get caught, I'm sure Mr. Hatch will toss the both of you out."

An image of her and Edgar riding his horse together floated before her eyes. She wondered how far the animal would be able to carry them.

Gertie quietly eased down from the wagon and snuggled beside Edgar. He slid over to make room for her, but she wanted to be close to him and so she pressed her body against his. She leaned over him and kissed him. Her breasts hung loosely under her chemise and they rested heavily on his chest. The kiss lasted a long, sensuous time. Her tongue touched his; tasting and savoring him. Gertie wanted to melt into his body.

Minutes later, her lips pulled away. Staring into his eyes, her hands slowly roamed over his body. Her body—her heart—ached for him.

This must be what love feels like.

She decided she was in love with Edgar, but she dare not say the words. She could not risk breaking the magical spell. Rolling onto her back, she lifted the hem of her nightdress and opened her legs.

Leaning over her, Edgar captured her lips. Tenderly, his tongue touched hers. She moaned as his kiss deepened. Clutching his face, her tongue met his almost feverish advance. Still kissing her, his hand cupped her left breast, squeezing and massaging her.

"Now, please," she moaned, "take me."

* * *

Laramie Mountain

Two days later, a purplish-blue smudge appeared on the horizon.

"That is the Laramie Mountain," Edgar said in answer to Gertie's inquiry. We will be at Fort John on the Laramie River in a few days."

"What, exactly, is there?"

"It is a trading post, much like the one I used to operate on the Canadian border. I've not yet been to this one, but I expect to find a mercantile store, blacksmith, and the likes. We will stay there for a couple of days so everyone can make what repairs they need."

And then you will leave me, she mused silently. She shrugged off the foul mood which permeated her soul. "Will there be a cobbler there?" She inched up her skirt and lifted her foot to show Edgar that she was wearing the moccasins which the Pawnee woman had given her. "My shoes fell into ruin and I discarded them."

"I expect so, but there will not be much in the way of fashion available."

Gertie snickered. "All I want is a good pair of sturdy shoes. I won't care what they look like."

"Looks like you could use a new skirt as well."

Gertie's skirt had been torn and patched so many times that it had begun to resemble something a child's doll might wear.

"Yes, but I've no money to buy either," she lamented.

"The Lord will provide. But for now, I must be off." Edgar touched the brim of his hat and nodded as he spurred his horse. Gertie watched as he rode toward the purple mountain.

The ground became hard and dry, and the Oregon Trail narrowed into a single pair of parallel wagon ruts. The wagon train no longer traveled as two rows of wagons, but they followed the ruts in a long single file. To save those in the back from perpetually eating the dust, the space between the wagons was increased. This allowed the wind to blow the dust of the lead wagons away. The wranglers permitted the livestock to graze over a broader range as the grass became scarce.

Gertie wondered how much worse the desert would be.

The mountain on the horizon grew larger as the days passed. Now an immense feature on the landscape, it beckoned the travelers forward ever faster. On July 3rd, Edgar did not ride ahead of the wagon train to perform his usual scout duties. Instead, he brought Mr. Smoot's horse to Gertie.

"The wagons will camp on this side of the Laramie River tonight, and cross over to Fort John in the morning. I thought you might like to ride ahead and see the place, such as it is."

"Indeed, I would!" Gertie was excited to have something different to do. Two months of plodding along beside the wagon had bored her to near tears.

Their horses trotted side-by-side in the parallel wagon wheel ruts. They passed several groups of three and four wagons which Gertie had no idea existed. She had failed to grasp how crowded the Oregon Trail was. The majority of the trains had been traveling at about the same speed so that their distance had maintained a sense of separation. At noontime they sat on their horses, resting on the crest a hill overlooking the settlement.

"Gertie, are you happy?"

Edgar's odd question surprised her. "Well..."

Gertie watched the wagons cross the Laramie River as she pondered an answer to his question. The valley below them was a sharp contrast to the desolate area they had just traversed. This land was green and fertile; a most beautiful expanse of country. The air was clear and dry, and she examined the distant mountains with surprising clarity. This river was shallower and slower moving than the Platte, however, it was a broad muddy expanse and the wagons struggled to cross it. The alabaster white of the adobe structure of Fort John sat on a bluff, above the river. Gertie spent quite some time staring at the fort; it was the first building she had seen since leaving Independence, Missouri.

"I mean..." Edgar paused again, unable to find the words to describe what he meant.

"I guess I'm happy," she said at length. "This is a hard venture and we struggle every day, all day long just to eke out a few miles closer to..." Her thoughts trail away as she struggled to recall where it was they were going. "To Oregon," she continued, "and only the Lord knows what we will find there. It is such an exhausting time. I've not paused to think about such things as happiness."

He nodded, but he did not spur his horse to continue their trip.

"What about you? Are you happy?" She turned to examine his eyes.

He wet his lips, and grinned. He wet his lips again.

"Yes, I am. I was just thinking, as we rode along together, about how happy I am. As I sit here on this horse, talking with you, Gertie, looking out on this vast, beautiful, untamed land—I am the happiest—the most content—that I've ever been." He looked away for a moment and then straight into her eyes. "I know this must sound strange as our current life is so hard. But," he inhaled a deep breath, "I find myself to be so delighted with the way things are working out."

"Well, yes, I am happy to be with you too," she said, but she still had no idea of exactly what he was saying.

He reached across the narrow gulf between them and squeezed her hand.

With a grunt, he urged his horse forward and turned his attention to the road ahead. Gertie's horse followed without waiting for her command and they descended the hill.

Edgar led them to a spot a hundred yards upstream of where the unfamiliar wagons were crossing. Dozens of wagons were camped on the south side of the river, waiting to cross. Long, thick ropes were stretched across the river to guide the wagons when they reached the deepest parts. Edgar ignored this and urged their horses to swim. While their horses had little difficulty in swimming through the deep spots, the wagons were having a great deal of difficulty. Gertie experienced the drag and pull of a wet, sodden skirt and almost lost her seating when her horse first lurched into a swimming motion. As the horses and their wet riders stumbled out of the water, she hiked her skirt higher to keep the wet hem from rubbing her legs raw as the horse walked.

"I'll have to help the wagons across tomorrow," Edgar said when they reached the dry bank. "But today we have a few hours to ourselves."

Edgar had not characterized the encampment as a town, and he had been correct. Fort John was an adobe building, smaller but still reminiscent of the European castles. Situated on a high bluff peninsula jutting out into a sharp bend in the river, the stockade with its defensive parapets stood guard over the Laramie River. A disorganized collection of canvas tents dotted the hillside to the north. To the south of the fort were throngs of Indian teepees along the Laramie River. The Indians did not appear to be a threat as they were equally interested in trading with the Oregon Trail travelers.

"This is a seasonal business," Edgar said. "Most of the trading is with the emigrants, but most of the wagons pass through in the space of a month. Think of it," he signed, "a thousand wagons pass this way in such a short time—roughly thirty a day. It's quite astounding."

Gertie nodded her understanding as she viewed the chaotic affair.

They rode past a campground with more than a hundred wagons. The sight reminded her of their start, months earlier, with wagons grouped on the field south of Independence. Inside the fort's walls Edgar led Gertie to the blacksmith shop and dismounted from his horse.

"Here, this man makes shoes," he said, as he gallantly helped her off her horse.

"Ah, Mr. Millar, I've been waiting for you." A cheerful, burly man greeted them. "Come right this way, young lady," he gestured to Gertie. He had her stand barefoot on patches of thick leather while he traced around her feet with a piece of charcoal. When he was done, he said, "Yes, yes, come back in two days. I'll have them ready for you, Missy."

Gertie hoped her ragged moccasins would last two more days.

"As a practical matter," she said to Edgar as they led their horses across the open courtyard, "how am I to pay for the shoes?"

He paused and appeared on the verge of embracing her, but held back. Gertie followed his gaze to where Mr. Hatch was talking with another man. Rees stood to one side, but was watching her.

"Don't worry about it. I said I would take care of you and I will pay for the shoes, and for material to make a new skirt as well," Edgar said, when his attention returned to Gertie.

"Thank you," Gertie said, knowing exactly how she wanted to repay him. She desperately wanted to kiss him, but dared not show her affections in front of Mr. Hatch.

They tied their horses to a railing and approached the mercantile shop.

"Mrs. Berg, indeed it is you."

Gertie turned to see the man Hatch and Rees had been talking with was none other than Major Jamison.

"Yes, Major Jamison, it is good to see you."

"Mr. Hatch was just this very minute telling me your sad tale. Please accept my condolences for the loss of your husband. Mr. Berg was a fine man."

"Thank you," Gertie could think of nothing more to say. She felt guilty standing beside Edgar; she had not thought of Peter in days.

"I was asking the Major if he could accept you and the other Protestants into his train," Mr. Hatch changed the subject. "That is, if you do not want to continue on to the Great Salt Lake."

Gertie looked back and forth between the two men. The issue at hand was: did she want to become a Mormon? The answer was: no. But she did want to continue in the direction of California. It seemed she needed to decide now, yet Edgar had not suggested that she could continue with him. She looked to Edgar and he nodded. Unsure of what he might know, or of exactly what his nod meant, she turned back to Major Jamison.

"Yes, sir, I am grateful you can accommodate me," she said.

Gertie gasped and froze.

"What's wrong?" Edgar asked. "You look like you've seen a ghost."

In a manner of speaking, she had seen a ghost. "That woman," Gertie pointed toward a woman exiting the store, "she is wearing my dress."

Edgar followed her stare and asked, "What do you mean?"

"I mean, I sewed that dress. I made it and she is wearing it!" Gertie found no words to describe how a woman intimately knew every stitch in the clothing she created. The large bow which formed the bustle was unmistakably her handicraft.

"Can you be mistaken? How could she get it?" Edgar asked.

Gertie's jaw worked and her face flushed with anger. "It was in my trunk on our wagon. The wagon Peter and I had. She stole it."

"She probably didn't steal it," Edgar countered. "However, she probably bought it from someone who did." Edgar watched the woman walk away. "Let's ask her."

"Who is this man?" Gertie heard Major Jamison ask Hatch.

"He is Mr. Millar, the one who rescued Mrs. Berg. While he claims to be an educated lawyer, I hired him as a scout," Hatch explained. "He does know the ways of the Indians."

Edgar and Gertie followed the woman out of the fort toward a collection of camped wagons. "Excuse me, madam," he said. "Might I inquire where you purchased that beautiful dress?" The woman stopped. She examined Edgar and Gertie.

Gertie suddenly felt ashamed. Standing in her mud stained blouse and ragged skirt she looked like a beggar.

"I didn't buy it, sir. I-I—" The woman stopped her speech as Jamison, Hatch, and Rees closed around her.

"You didn't buy it? Then please tell us, how did you come by it?" Edgar's voice morphed into his lawyer persona.

"I-I—"

"Yes, please tell us. It is rather important," Mr. Hatch encouraged.

"My husband's brother, he gave it to me."

"I see. And what is your brother-in-law's name?"

"Uh, Harry Bloomfield."

"Mrs. Bloomfield, do you know where Harry bought the dress?" Edgar pressed.

"He-he found it. It was in a trunk someone discarded along the trail."

"Discarded!" Gertie erupted. "I did *not* discard the trunk, it was stolen. That's *my* dress!"

Edgar placed a consoling hand on Gertie's shoulder to quiet her while he continued to address Mrs. Bloomfield. "Madam, could you take us to your brother-in-law so we can learn about the details of how he found the trunk?"

"He's over there," she pointed to a cluster of four wagons.

"That," Gertie hissed into Edgar's ear, "is our wagon! See, it's smaller than the other wagons." Suddenly, Gertie gasped and her knees buckled. Edgar reached for her arms to support her. She pointed to a man approaching from the river carrying a bucket of water, he limped slightly. "That is the man, see the scar? He is the one who murdered Peter."

Edgar examined the man's lean physique. The scar along the left side of his chin was clearly visible and matched Gertie's earlier description.

"You're sure? You are certain, that is the man?" Edgar asked.

"Yes, absolutely. He shot Peter in the head and stole our wagon." She pointed as the man poured the water from the bucket into the barrel strapped to the wagon.

"The oxen are already yoked," Edgar said. "They are getting ready to leave." Edgar stood silent for a long moment. He reached down to release the leather strap which held his revolver in its holster. "Mr. Hatch, the day Gertie and I arrived in your camp you said you would hang the man responsible for her husband's death, if you could get your hands on him. Now it seems the good Lord has delivered him into your grasp."

Jamison, Hatch, and Rees approached the man along one side of the wagon. Edgar came up behind him from the opposite side. As the startled Harry Bloomfield examined the three men advancing upon him, Edgar jerked Bloomfield's revolver from its holster and pressed its barrel into his back.

Edgar did not cock the pistol's hammer, but he did snarl in Bloomfield's ear. "You are under arrest for the murder of Peter Berg on the night of June thirteenth." Edgar gripped the man's collar and pushed him forward.

"What-what—"

Rees produced a leather strap and bound Bloomfield's hands behind his back.

"What is the meaning of this?" Bloomfield found his voice and shouted. "You can't arrest me."

"I dare say, we can, Mr. Bloomfield," Major Jamison stated. "True, there is no formal law enforcement in the territories. However, we citizens are righteous. We require no code of laws other than the moral code enacted by our Creator and which is found in the heart of every decent man. We won't allow murderers to walk free among us."

"I didn't kill anyone." Bloomfield turned to another man. "Tell them Andrew; tell them that I'm with you."

"This is my brother—" Andrew Bloomfield started to explain

Interrupting, Edgar said, "He will get his chance to explain his side of the story."

"You are the lawyer here," Hatch said to Edgar. "How do we proceed?"

A throng of over twenty people had gathered and Gertie wondered whose side they might be on.

"What's going on?" she heard one voice say.

"What did he do?"

"He's a murderer."

"They're gonna lynch him."

Gertie's stomach churned and she stooped to retch. Someone reached out to support her.

"Go find twelve men who don't know either Harry Broomfield or Gertrude Berg. We'll hold a trial," Edgar announced.

Hatch nodded toward Rees, and he scurried to poll the onlookers. In the ten minutes it took to gather twelve citizens, the crowd surrounding them grew to a hundred people. It seemed to Gertie that everyone in the Fort John encampment gathered to watch.

Edgar released Bloomfield to stand alone. "This woman, Gertrude Berg of Cincinnati, has accused this man, Harry Broomfield of murdering her husband, Peter Berg, on the night of June thirteenth. As the only one in these parts with legal training, I will direct this court. You men," Edgar swept his arm across the gathered jury, "will stand in judgment. Your verdict will be the law here."

"I didn't do—"

Edgar poked Bloomfield in the gut—hard. "You will get your chance to speak." Edgar put his arm around Gertie and gently led her into the circle. "Mrs. Berg, is it true you and your husband were members of Major Jamison's wagon train when you left Independence?"

Gertie looked between Edgar and Bloomfield. Her gaze surveyed the crowd and settled on Major Jamison. "Yes." She did her best to speak clearly, without hesitation.

"And when your wagon was damaged, did Major Jamison instruct your husband to turn back?"

"Yes."

"And when you stopped for the night, when you went to the river to fetch water, did you hear a gunshot?"

"Yes."

"Can you tell us what you saw when you returned to your camp?"

"Yes, I saw that man—"

"Let the record show that Mrs. Berg has identified the defendant, Mr. Harry Bloomfield," Edgar said before realizing no one was recording the proceedings. "Uh, please continue."

"Yes, that man was standing over the body of my husband, Peter. I hid in the bushes and watched as he stole Peter's money belt, and then took all of his clothes. He then whipped our oxen," Gertie pointed to the nearby wagon and its yoke of oxen, "and took them across the river."

"How are you certain this is the man?"

"He has the same scar on his face. And, she is wearing my dress!" Gertie pointed to the woman they had first approached.

"Madam," Edgar guided Mrs. Bloomfield into the circle, "please tell us how you came to own this dress."

"He-he gave it to me." She pointed toward Harry Bloomfield. "He said he found it in a trunk discarded along the trail."

"Mrs. Berg, can you describe your trunk where you had stored your dress?"

"Yes. It was about so big," she estimated its dimensions with her hands, "and black with red trim. Our names were carved into its top surface."

"Someone search the wagon and see if there is such a trunk inside," Edgar commanded, and two men hastily moved to comply. In a few moments, they produced the trunk and set it down in the circle. "Gentlemen of the jury, please note that the names of Peter and Gertrude Berg can be seen in the surface of the lid, however someone has attempted to scratch them out."

The twelve men examined the trunk and nodded.

"Now, Mr. Bloomfield, do you wear a money belt?"

"What?"

Edgar signaled to Rees and he pulled up Bloomfield's shirt to reveal a money belt. Rees pulled the belt loose and handed it to Edgar. He examined it before passing it to the jury.

"Mrs. Berg, what was your late husband's middle name?"

"Uh, it-it's Anthony."

"Will the jury notice that the initials embroidered in the money belt are P-A-B, which are the initials of Mr. Peter Anthony Berg," Edgar stated confidently, and waited for the crowd to settle before continuing. "I contend to the jury, it has been proven beyond a doubt that this man, Harry Bloomfield, did murder Peter Berg and steal the belongings of Mrs. Gertrude Berg." The crowd again churned and grumbled angrily causing Edgar to fire a pistol shot into the air to silence them. "Mr. Bloomfield, you may now express your position."

Harry Bloomfield examined the faces of the jury. The attentive stares did not waver from his eyes. "I didn't - did not murder anyone. I found the trunk along the trail."

"And the wagon?" Edgar questioned.

"Uh—"

"Mr. Millar, might I add a comment?" Major Jamison called out.

"Of course, sir."

"I wish the jury to know that I keep careful records of the brands on the livestock in my wagon train. I can testify, without a doubt, the double-hat brand on those oxen," he pointed toward the yoked team, "was on the team which Mr. Peter Berg purchased in Independence."

"It was somebody else who done the killing. I found the wagon, that's all," Bloomfield focused on his defense.

"Mrs. Berg, would you again state for the jury the description of the man you saw standing over your husband's lifeless body?"

"Yes," Gertie reiterated the description which matched that of Bloomfield.

"I will now ask the jury to consider the evidence and testimony here and announce their verdict," Edgar gestured to the gathered twelve men.

Nodding their understanding, they gathered together and deliberated the fate of the accused. A mere minute later, one man turned and announced, "We find this man, Harry Bloomfield, guilty of murder with a decree of death."

"Get a rope," a voice shouted from the crowd.

There being no tree available, two wagons were positioned nose-to-nose and the tongues of their hitches were bound together. As the wagons were pushed closer together, the tongues reached into the air to form a tall 'A' frame. A hangman's noose was suspended from the top. Bloomfield was placed upon an unsaddled horse, facing backwards. The noose was placed around his neck.

"Do you wish to meet your maker without confessing your sins?" a preacher approached the convicted man.

"I-I," he turned to face Gertie, "I beg for your forgiveness."

The crowd silenced and all eyes were upon the young widow.

Gertie thought of Peter and his dreams of a farm in Oregon. She shook her head and turned her gaze to the ground.

"May God forgive you and welcome you into his arms," the preacher concluded.

Major Jamison slapped the horse's rump and it jumped away to leave Bloomfield hanging. Gertie did not look up.

From its beginning to its end, the entire business lasted no more than two hours.

Gertie turned into Edgar's embrace and wept.

Someone handed her the money belt with Peter's initials. "I want my things," she spoke sharply. She raised her face and shouted, "I want my wagon and team back. I want all that was stolen." Gertie's eyes fell to the woman wearing her dress.

"You can keep it. I don't want the dress." Gertie turned to Andrew Bloomfield. "What of his wife? What will become of her?"

"If she ever learns of this, I expect she'll rejoice. My brother was a bad man and he beat her. His wife left him two years ago." He turned and spat into the ground. "It was she that gave him that scar."

CHAPTER ELEVEN

July 3, 1848
Fort John on the Laramie River

Rees and several other men ushered Gertie's wagon into Major Jamison's camp. After collecting their horses, Edgar and Gertie followed the wagon the quarter mile to the encampment. Climbing down from her horse, Gertie was confronted by the wagon master.

"We are leaving in the morning," Major Jamison told Gertie. "Will you be ready?"

"Yes." As weary of travel as she was, she was ready to leave Fort John and the awful business behind her.

"Mr. Hatch has returned to his wagon train to express my offer to the other Protestants. If they accept, their wagons will be brought across the river this evening." He paused for a moment to consider his next words. "Mr. Millar said he will be driving your wagon, if that is acceptable to you?"

Gertie nodded. She was glad to hear Edgar would remain by her side. She had expected it, but she was confused how this worked into his plan to go to California. Major Jamison's train was heading to Oregon Territory. Standing alone beside her wagon, Gertie studied it for a moment. She recalled how proud Peter had been of it, and how it had been their faithful home. Sighing, she climbed aboard and diverting her mind to the task at hand. She began sifting through the contents of her wagon. Those items she didn't recognize as hers, she tossed out the back end.

"Gertie," Edgar called to her.

"Yes?" She poked her head through the canvas cover.

"I'm going back with Mr. Rees now. I'll be helping Mrs. Clark and Mrs. Howe cross the river, and then I'll return here."

"Thank you." Reaching through the canvas opening, she leaned close to Edgar, touched his face and looked into his eyes. "Edgar, thank you for everything." Seeming to understand the fullness of her meaning, he nodded. "You might not want to throw all this away." He gestured to the pile of goods she had tossed. "We will need items to trade for food and supplies along the way."

We, yes, we will need supplies.

Gertie watched him ride away, trailing Mr. Smoot's horse. She climbed down onto the cluttered ground covered by the debris she had tossed from within. Looking closely and with careful consideration, she repacked the items which appeared to have trading value.

Gertie took water from the bucket attached to the wagon and filled a pan. The cold water felt invigorating as she cleansed herself of the dirt, the day and her thoughts of who had occupied her wagon. As she washed her face and changed into fresh clothes from her trunk, she was surprised to find her own clothing more or less undisturbed. Since her new shoes would not be ready for two days, she contemplated donning her church shoes which were still in the trunk. However, she didn't want to risk ruining them in the dirt pathways of Fort John. So, she put the worn moccasins back on. Holding her breath, she dug into the bottom of the trunk. She opened the hidden compartment. The ten American Gold Eagle ten-dollar coins were still there. Gertie sighed with relief to once again have the hundred dollars her father had presented as her dowry. Harry Bloomfield had not found the money. Apparently, he had given her trunk little thought in his rush to steal the wagon. She counted out another forty dollars in miscellaneous gold and silver coins. In Peter's money belt, she found an additional eighteen dollars.

A hundred and fifty-eight dollars!

Gertie was relieved she was no longer destitute, living off the mercy of others. She took off her wedding ring and placed it with the coins. She repacked the trunk, concealing the false bottom. In the peace and quiet she had not known for the past month, she collected her writing materials. Slowly, she drafted a letter to Peter's parents telling them of his demise and the justice that had been handed down to his killer. She wrote a similar letter to her own parents. To this letter she added that she was continuing westward, and on to California, escorted by a gentleman, Edgar Millar. Gertie added that she believed Edgar would ask for her hand in marriage. She went on to proclaim that Edgar had saved her life and without him she would not have survived this arduous Oregon Trail. She told them of deaths suffered by others and also of the widows who remained to finish the trip on their own. Gertie wanted them to understand Edgar was a principled man and could be trusted as her companion for the remainder of her travels. She closed the letter promising to write again.

"Mrs. Berg?" Gertie heard the familiar voice of Mrs. Jamison.

"Hello." Gertie climbed down from the wagon and embraced the woman. "I am so very glad to be back in your company." Gertie briefly related her adventures and accepted Mrs. Jamison's invitation to supper.

Gertie handed the two letters to the wagonmaster. "Major, I've written Peter's and my parents. Could you see that these are placed with the mail heading eastward?"

"Of course, ma'am."

"And here, sir, I insist on paying my way." She handed him twenty dollars in loose coins. "This is what remained in my husband's money belt." It was a small lie; she did not see the need to pay the full $50. That money would be necessary to give her a new start or to give both her and Edgar a start if they did indeed marry. So the little financial indiscretion seemed justified. A widow must be cautious.

The Major first attempted to refuse the money, but seeing the determination in Gertie's eyes, he accepted it.

When they had finished eating, Beth, Grace, and the other two wagons which had been attacked by the Indians arrived with Edgar.

"Gertie, Grace tells me they have a bathhouse in town. Would you like to join us?" Beth asked.

Gertie saw she had Mrs. Clark and another woman in tow. The third woman was a young bride, Rosalie. She and her husband, Charlie, were among the Protestants who were changing from Mr. Hatch's wagon train to Major Jamison's.

Gertie turned to study Fort John. She wondered if she should show her face in the town. While late in the day, the midsummer sun was still above the horizon, and she didn't want to be recognized.

"I don't know—"

"I've slept with ya. I know. Come on dreary, you need a bath as bad as the rest of us and this will be our last opportunity for a long while."

Beth tugged on her hand and Gertie allowed herself to be swept along with the other three women. The thought of a full body bath with soap and possibly warm water, took all fears and concerns out of her thoughts.

While it had been possible to bathe in the rivers and streams along the way, most women had shunned the opportunities. The majority of the plains was wide open, offering no privacy. Additionally, they would not have been safe unless guarded by the men folk. While married women could accept the protection and privacy offered by their husbands, the unmarried women could not.

Gertie had not bathed since the South Platte River crossing.

Men lined up to bathe in the Laramie River. However, west of the stockade a large tent had been erected as a bathhouse for the women.

"How much you pay?" a Chinese woman asked in her singsong version of English. Gertie had never seen a Chinese woman before, but she recognized her features from drawings she had seen.

The woman rapped her long nails on a sign. Reading it, the four women learned that each tub of water was used four times. The first bather paid a quarter-dollar while each subsequent bather paid a nickel less than the one before.

"I think we deserve clean water," Grace said and plopped down a silver dollar. "My treat for all of you." The other three women profusely thanked her. "No," she shunned their expressions, "this is my way of thanking y'all for all the support you've given me for the past two weeks."

After waiting until four of the tubs had been used four times, the women were ushered into the big tent. From the inside, the building was a wooden frame with the walls and ceiling fashioned from sheets of white canvas. Gertie was reminded of the huge sails which had propelled her ship to America.

They undressed while Chinese women dumped and refilled the tubs. They eased their dusty, weary bodies into the wonderfully clean warm water. While not hot, it was pleasingly tepid. They took their time washing with the real soap; they got their money's worth. Finally, they dried their bodies with real towels before dressing.

It was twilight when they stepped onto the street. There were very few women about, but several men were coming and going from the largest tent in the encampment. Piano music could be heard radiating from the makeshift building.

"Who's up for a drink?" Grace asked, and headed toward the saloon.

"I'm with you," Beth said and Rosalie silently followed.

"I didn't bring any money," Gertie said. She didn't indicate how much money she had left behind in her wagon. It was with a sense of hesitation that she stood for a moment, considering the direction the unescorted women were headed.

"Don't worry, I'll lend you some." Beth took her hand to drag her along.

Entering the saloon, they noticed they were not the only women in the big room. However, they were the only women full dressed. There were a half-dozen women sporting about in their undergarments. They wore black boots and stockings with short red underskirts—barely covering their knees. They had nothing more than a tight red bodice to cover their bosoms. These women were drinking and talking with the men; two of the women were actually sitting and squirming teasingly in two lucky men's laps. The remaining men were mostly engaged in standing at the bar drinking or sitting at the tables playing a card game which Gertie suspected was faro. The men nearest the door stopped talking and stared at them.

"Oh, my word!" Gertie turned to leave, but Beth did not let go of her hand.

"Come on," she said, and pulled Gertie inside.

"Let's sit over here." Grace led them to a table on the opposite side of the room from the piano player. Leaving them, she strode up to the bar and returned with a bottle of amber fluid and four small glasses. She poured them each a measure and held her glass up in the air. "A toast, to the halfway point."

The women clinked their glasses and sipped their whiskey. Gertie had tasted whiskey before and she didn't like it. Nonetheless, she found herself drinking too much as she laughed with her friends. She found herself forgetting the turmoil and agony which the day had brought. The alcohol relaxed her.

"Are you going to marry Edgar?" Grace asked.

"I don't know. He hasn't asked me—yet," Gertie replied.

"You needn't worry what others might think about the short time since your husband's death," she continued. "This is a very hard land and a woman has little means to support herself, alone. The land in Oregon is only available to men. You would be a fool to let such a fine man as Mr. Millar go."

"Yes," Beth added, with a wink. "You should do what is necessary to make him happy." Feminine giggles followed that untoward comment as the widows agreed.

The four women sipped their whiskey and chuckled. Gertie knew exactly what Beth meant.

"We three widows should all find new husbands as quickly as possible. It is the only way for us to survive," Grace concluded.

Looking around the room, Gertie recognized two of the men at the bar to be wranglers with Major Jamison's wagon train. Of course, none of the Mormons were there. Gertie studied the men as they interacted with the women. She noticed how men would occasionally drift through the doorway beside the bar. A woman, taking one or two men by the hand, would lead them to the space behind the bar's back wall. Later, they would reappear. However, when the men returned, they came back alone with the women following after a few minutes.

"What's back there?" Gertie's curiosity got the best of her.

"Must be the latrines," Beth said.

Grace giggled and slurred something unintelligible.

"I could use a trip to the facilities." Beth stood.

"Me too." Rosalie joined her, and Gertie followed.

The three young women walked across the room, followed by the stares of most everyone there, and passed through the opening in the canvas wall. They walked along the canvas lined hallway for half a dozen yards, and then made a right turn. This revealed another hallway. However, the walls were not taut sheets of canvas; they were more like tent flaps. Opening one of the flaps, Gertie did not find a privy. The tiny room contained only a narrow cot.

Gertie turned to her friends. "What is this place?"

A sudden lull in the noise from the bar allowed them to hear sounds from one of the closed spaces. They heard the distinctive sounds of flesh upon flesh and a mixture of male and female moans that could only have originated from two people in the midst of carnal relations—and probably unmarried, based on what they had seen in the main common area of the saloon.

"We are in the wrong place!" Beth turned to leave.

Gertie was drawn to a different, softer sound from the room behind the second closed flap. She stepped closer and positioned her eye to peer through the crack. Inside the tiny room, she saw a man lying on the cot. His trousers were bunched at his knees while a woman knelt beside him.

"Oh, my word! We are *definitely* in the wrong place."

Gertie heard a quick *whoosh* as Rosalie peered over her shoulder and sucked in a breath.

"Are you here to earn some money?" Both young women turned to see one of the saloon girls standing behind them.

"No-no, we are looking for the latrine," Rosalie stammered. Beth was nowhere in sight.

The woman, slightly older than Gertie with coal black hair, chuckled. "This is certainly the wrong place for that." She eyed them up and down. "Well then, ya had best be on yer way." She stood aside and Gertie would have bolted except that Rosalie remained rooted in her path.

"What do you mean—make some money?" Rosalie asked.

"With the men." The saloon girl jerked her head toward the couple behind the canvas wall. Seeing the blank look that still remained on Rosalie's face, she added, "As ladies of the night. Ya know—prostitutes."

Gertie had read several passages in the Bible about prostitutes, but she had never known what the word meant. Now, she understood. "Women who have sex for money?" she asked, before realizing she was speaking aloud.

"Yes, lassie," the prostitute chuckled. "You *do* know what it is men want from women, don't ya?"

"Of course," Rosalie held up her left hand. "I'm married."

The canvas flap flew open and Edgar materialized, filling the doorway.

"What's this?" he exclaimed. "Just what is going on here?"

Gertie and Rosalie stared at him, slack jaw.

"No harm, sir," the prostitute calmly said to fill the silence. "We were just talking."

"*Talking?*" Edgar spat the word out as though it was a criminal act. He looked into Gertie's eyes. "Talking," he said again, softer but with the arching of one brow.

Gertie and Rosalie nodded in unison.

"This is no place for you, Gertie." He gripped her wrist and pulled her out of the back room business area. Turning, he fastened his other hand upon Rosalie's wrist. "You too. I'll take you back to your wagon."

Like two errant school children captured by the truant officer, Edgar led the women back to the saloon. Gertie saw that the table where Grace and Beth should have been waiting was empty.

"I sent them on ahead," Edgar stated. All eyes were on the young women as he paraded them to the door and out onto the street. "Do you two have any idea how dangerous that was?"

Gertie imagined there were lots of dangerous parts surrounding their evening, but she did not choose to focus upon any specific one. However, she was sure he would narrate a litany of the hazards later when they were alone.

Rosalie's husband, Charlie, met them as they entered the camp. Edgar released Rosalie as Charlie scooped her up and tossed her over his shoulder. She did not struggle or scream as he carried her to their wagon and to her fate.

"Oh, no," Gertie exclaimed as Edgar bent to press his shoulder against her belly. "No—no!" But it was too late. He hoisted her up like a sack of feed. She dangled down his back, as he carried her to their wagon.

Edgar lifted her up, over the back edge of the wagon and set her feet down. Peering over his shoulder, she saw a half-dozen men and women watching; their faces pale in the moonlight.

OH, no, not an audience!

With all Gertie's belongings piled inside the wagon, there was only a small empty place to stand at the back end. She moved aside as far as possible amongst the chaos of her possessions and Edgar hoisted himself over the edge. He closed and tied the canvas covering and lit a candle.

She sucked in a deep breath. "I won't ever do it again. No more saloons—ever. I promise."

"It's not just that. There is no way for me to list all the dangers to be found on this journey. You can't risk testing each hazard and then promising to never do them again. You need to begin using your brain and think about situations as they arise. Use your common sense judgment and avoid the dangerous ways."

She reasoned he was correct. She should have had the good sense to run as soon as she realized it was not the loo.

Silently, she nodded, and whispered, "Yes, Edgar, I promise, I will."

Suddenly, his expression changed. The anger on his face morphed into something else—something devilish.

"Take your dress off," Edgar commanded.

His words shocked her, slightly, but Gertie reached behind her back and fumbled with the buttons until the material slid down her legs.

"The underskirt too."

She pulled the free end of the ribbon which held the waistband tight. As the knot slipped loose, this fabric also pooled around her ankles.

He lifted her torso such that she was sitting on her trunk. She lay back onto the pallet of canvas. She hooked her heels behind his thighs and pulled him closer.

"Please, the candle," she whispered, and he blew it out.

Edgar pushed her chemise up higher and kissed her belly button. Moaning, she worked her fingers into his hair. Her tugs on his hair became more urgent as his kisses trailed lower.

"Oh, my God!" she cried, before silencing herself. She would be doubly embarrassed by entertaining the crowd more than she already had. "Please... don't stop," she whispered, as she received the tongue lashing Beth had described.

CHAPTER TWELVE

July 4, 1848
The desert

Gertie was happy the following morning. She wondered if the others could tell by looking at her what had gone on the night before. Suddenly, it dawned on her, she didn't care. Not one whit! Well, maybe a tad, but not enough to suffer chagrin for the evening's activities. As she began to recall the interaction between herself and Edgar, she realized she had reached an understanding of the dangers he had stressed. The adventurous nature that had been her lifelong challenge would not make her as tame as he seemed to want. However, she understood the need to be careful and grudgingly admitted to herself that Edgar was trying to keep her safe. Now, far away from the critical eyes of the Mormons, she drank coffee and openly kissed Edgar.

Coffee cups were emptied and stored away for the day's travels. Taking her seat in the wagon box, the wagon lurched forward. Despite the hard, jarring seat of the bouncing wagon, she rode instead of walking. Her new shoes would not be ready for another day, and her moccasins were mere scraps of leather, leaving her effectively barefoot. She sat and watched while Edgar drove their oxen to pull their wagon westward.

Our wagon, she mused. *Yes, I am very happy.*

For the first time since marrying Peter, she felt in control of her life's direction. She chuckled to herself, acknowledging she really had no control at all. Life on the Oregon Trail had shown her that. There was no choice but to plod onward. There was no possibility of stopping or turning around, but this was where she wanted to be and what she wanted to do—to plod onward with Edgar.

Heading northwest along the North Platte River from Fort John, the terrain became savage with never ending steep rocky hills. The Oregon Trail was, in most places, a single pair of parallel wagon wheel ruts. All of the emigrants stayed in these ruts as much as possible, trying to use this one trail with the wagons lined end to end as far as she could see in either direction. Their progress was slow; the line could travel no faster than its slowest affiliate. An unwritten rule of the road forbade a wagon from attempting to overtake another. The constant, slow, drudging motion of the oxen's feet and the turning of the wagon wheels created a cloud of dust which consumed them. If it hadn't been for the perpetual wind, the dust would have choked them all to death. Even with the help of the wind, they needed to further protect themselves. Each wore a kerchief tied over his or her nose and mouth. At night they simply stopped where they were and camped beside their wagon.

Gertie ignored all of these tribulations. She had her traveling home, her clothes, and she had Edgar. The next day went quickly and she found herself driving the team, her team. As promised, Edgar rode his horse back to Fort John and retrieved her new shoes. Gertie was still combing the dust from her hair when Edgar had returned. The shoes were crafted to her expectations. She smiled when she saw they were sturdy and fit her feet perfectly. However, no matter how carefully she stepped, the first day of walking was uncomfortable. When the wagons stopped for a break at midday, Edgar obtained a small container of mink oil and advised her to oil the insides to make them more flexible. As she sat at the back entrance of the wagon, ministering to her tired feet, Edgar watched her, smiling. Climbing into the cozy interior of the wagon bed, he stooped to lift each foot and massage it.

Bliss! Ah, such bliss. I've not felt such delight since... Ah, since last night.

Gertie giggled. With the lunch break finished, Edgar left the wagon and she donned the transformed shoes. The rest of the day was less painful and she was surprised at how quickly the shoes softened and became much more comfortable than they had been earlier in the day.

As the wagon train progressed, the line of mountains which began with the Laramie Peak grew closer. With the assistance of a teenage boy, Gertie once again took charge of driving the oxen. The young boy kept them trudging at a quicker, more focused pace than she had been able to do previously. Her increasing ability to drive the team, freed Edgar to resume his daily hunting. The population of buffalo diminished and the constant line of people and wagons had frightened the game into the hills. Yet, Edgar never failed to bring home a deer or an antelope. In doing this, he was not working as a scout for Major Jamison, but as her provider. Bearing in mind the need of those who had no hunters, he always brought sufficient meat to feed the merry widows and several others. His thoughtfulness for others endeared Edgar even more to her heart. She would watch as he delivered the extra meat to the different wagons and welcome him back with a broad smile. He was an effective provider, in many ways.

"Edgar and the Merry Widows," Major Jamison had called them. Almost immediately this was what everyone else called them as well. Gertie lived with Edgar as a wife lived with her husband. If any of the members of their traveling troupe remembered Peter, and thought evil of her, they kept their thoughts to themselves. No one said a disparaging word to her.

After a hundred miles of the rugged terrain, the long line of wagons paused to rest the oxen and the people who tended them.

"The river bends here to the south," Edgar said. "We must cross it to continue heading west." He concentrated on the horizon. She knew he had studied John C. Fremont's maps, in the Great Pathfinder guidebook, and she imagined he was mentally plotted the trail ahead.

While the river had shrunk to a fraction of its former size, its churning, dark water remained a formidable adversary. In the steep terrain of the low mountains, the Platte River was not the peaceful, slow moving waterway they had crossed a month earlier. From a hilltop, they gazed down on an encampment of wagons beside the river. Gertie watched as one wagon was ferried across.

"The river here is too deep to be crossed," Edgar continued. "So, the Mormon settlers living nearby have set up a ferry. They charge a pretty penny to carry the wagons across, but the alternative is to travel several days south to find a shallow crossing." Thomas pointed to the line of wagons stretching southward. "Major Jamison has paid for us to graze our livestock here and to cross."

Gertie studied the contrast between the green grass along the river and the dull gray sagebrush beyond it, to the west.

"And that," she pointed westward, "is that the desert?"

"Yes, when we leave here, there will be several days of travel with little water. Or at least that is what Major Jamison has said. I've not ventured across the river. Then there will be two hundred miles of desolate land to cross. However, there will be springs and streams to provide us with water for most of it."

Two days later, the wagons were all across the river. Each of them felt relief after the dangerous maneuvering and were not the least bit sad when they left the sight of the North Platte River for the last time. They set out before the sun had risen. They filled every barrel to the brim, but this water was for the oxen. Dry travel was before them and the oxen would need the water to stay strong as they pulled the wagons through the arid land. Thus, they were instructed not to drink the barreled water themselves.

Progressing, ever forward, the weary settlers crossed through the most rugged hills that they had yet encountered followed by mile after mile of rock and sand. Only the prickly pear cactus, rabbit brush, and sparse sagebrush managed to grow there. At last, they reached a spring and rejoined the emigrants who had not crossed on the ferry. Gertie's path had been several days shorter. Even considering how difficult the terrain had been, theirs had been the safer path. She learned of the death of one family when their wagon tumbled while crossing the river. Danger lurked everywhere and what seemed easy could suddenly become difficult. Tragedy had blossomed several times along the rutted Oregon Trail.

For the next three days, the pioneers continued across the desert. They camped wherever they found water, even if they had traveled a mere handful of miles. Five days after leaving the Platte River, they had traveled only 50 miles, but they reached the Sweetwater River. Gertie found it to be aptly named; she had never tasted such delicious water. They camped for a day of rest beside a giant rock.

"This is known as Independence Rock. Major Jamison says the settlers carve their names in it as they pass by," Edgar said.

They walked to the monolith jutting from the desert floor and studied some of the names and dates. Gertie observed it was not single, continuous granite rock. Its surface had broken in numerous places, leaving fissures between jumbled boulders. The windblown sand had worn the exposed surfaces smooth and had collected in the crevices.

"Come on, it is an easy climb," Edgar urged her as they worked their way around and over and around the individual boulders which created the huge granite monolith. They climbed higher. "Look there, isn't it stunning," he said, pointing to the horizon.

Gertie shaded her eyes from the sun and scanned the horizon where the azure sky met the dusty brown earth. Edgar pulled her close and she melted against his side.

"It's breathtaking," she said, enjoying the closeness of their bodies while she studied the purplish mounds of distant mountains.

They found an unused space on the monolith's surface. Pulling borrowed tools from his belt, Edgar carved their names on a flat rock worn smooth by the wind. She silently watched as the letters materialized: Edgar and Gertie Millar, July 1848. He carved a heart around their names. She watched patiently and quietly until he had finished the task of immortalizing them on this stone.

Her breath caught in her chest and she found it difficult to speak. She pointed to their entwined names carved into the rock.

"What does this mean?" she stammered. Pointing to their names, she drew her finger under the word 'Millar' after hers.

"Well...well, it just seemed to be more appropriate than Berg, and I don't know your maiden name."

"It's Hengel," she said. "But I like this better." She sighed and added, "So much better." She sighed and added, "so much better."

She traced her finger along the letters, and the heart that surrounded them.

She smiled, think how much she adored his artwork. She kissed him. Locating a patch of soft sand between two boulders, hidden from the view of those below, they laid down. As they lay facing one another, Edgar cradled her head and held her as he kissed her, softly at first, and then with an urgent passion. She opened her lips and their tongues touched, explored, and danced.

Moments passed and Edgar lifted her dress. With no hesitation, he found that for which he searched and his fingers twirled her thick curly hairs. His stimulation of her lady parts was immediate and intense. She bucked and arched her back, giving herself over to him. Reaching down, she helped him lower his trousers. Slowly, in the cool shadows, they made love.

As his climax approached, he did the oddest thing. He pressed deeper into her. They had made love many times in the weeks before, and each time he had withdrawn before his culmination. This time he let his seed fill her. Gertie wrapped her arms around him and gripped his hips with her knees as they climaxed together.

While she hoped the act had been some sort of consummation of an unwritten marriage contract, she said nothing about it. They climbed back down off the rock and walked hand in hand back to the wagons.

Day after day, the slow moving wagons followed the Sweetwater River. As they were traveling upstream, the river's girth shrank a slight amount each day. Due to its never ending twists and turns, they crossed it six times. These crossings were simple and had none of the potential tragedy of the previous rivers. There was rich, green grass along the riverbanks for the livestock. However, the land a few hundred yards away was nothing but rocks and sand interspersed with thin wisps of sagebrush. Even the rabbit brush could not take hold here. Sagebrush, apparently, could grow anywhere. They allowed their livestock to range free. The animals would not venture far out of sight of the only water available.

The wagon trains had drifted apart as various small groups stopped to witness the miracle of a new birth or to take a much-needed break. All too often, they stopped to bury one of their party who had died. Gertie had given up counting the graves they passed.

CHAPTER THIRTEEN

July 30, 1848
Tragedy strikes

"What was that?" Beth cried out.

Gertie, Beth, and Grace had been cooking a meal to share. Edgar was hunting; he had not been successful for the past two days and they were digging deep into their supply of dried meats.

"It was a gunshot!" Grace replied.

Gertie's blood ran ice-cold and chills went up her spine.

"Maybe someone shot a snake," she said, wishing this was all that it meant. With Edgar out late, her mind raced through a number of frightening meanings the shot could have. Indian attack was the first idea which came to her mind, but they hadn't seen any Indians since leaving the Platte River.

Shouts sang out several wagons away, and the three women raced to see the source of the commotion.

"It's Mr. Sager. He shot himself," a woman told them. In horror, the women watched the agony on the man's face as other men examined him. They tried valiantly to help him as blood spurted from his leg.

"Someone get the child away," a man pointed to Sager's ten year old daughter as she approached.

Gertie, not wanting the girl to see any more of the man's plight, gently but adamantly took the girl's hand and lead her back to Gertie's wagon.

"I'm sure your father will be just fine." Gertie attempted to console the child. "They will patch him up, but we don't want to get in the way." The girl said nothing, but appeared unconvinced. Gertie remembered having been told that the girl's mother died of a fever somewhere east of Fort John. As this was during the time Gertie was with the Mormons, she had not witnessed the event. However, she understood why the girl was not easily swayed to believe her father would recover.

Gertie searched her memory for the girl's name. "Catherine, I'm Gertie. Could you please, help me finish cooking dinner? There is so much to do."

The girl nodded. Gertie assigned some tasks to her and prayed.

Edgar returned from hunting. As he had been the day before, he was empty handed. Seeing the turmoil, he joined the others around Mr. Sager. A short while later, he approached Gertie. Gertie held the girl, covering her face. Edgar shook his head and gazed into the fire with a haggard look on his face.

"He—he was removing his pistol from its holster and," he swallowed the lump in his throat, "and dropped it. It fired and shot him in the groin. The ball passed all through his insides. There was nothing to be done."

Gertie held the girl while she sobbed. An hour of grief stunning hysteria had exhausted the child. As Catherine began to quiet, Gertie took the youngster to bed with her and held the child until they both fell asleep.

In the morning, a tent was set up and Mr. Sager's body was laid out for Catherine to say her last goodbye. They carried his body to a grave a quarter mile from the Oregon Trail such that future travelers would not risk traveling over it. His name was carved into a wooden headboard, which was all that could be done. Major Jamison read from the Bible and the women sang hymns. At the end of it, everyone returned to the wagons. They were too mournful to pick up stakes and carry-on, so a day of mourning was announced.

"Mr. Millar," Major Jamison approached them, "ma'am," he tipped his hat to Gertie. He looked at the girl nestled in her arms. "Miss Catherine," he said as he removed his hat. "We are all so very sorry about what has happened." He turned to Edgar. "May I ask you to walk with me?"

Gertie watched the two men moved out of earshot and conversed.

"The Major has asked that we take charge of the girl." Edgar said when he returned. "It seems she has no one and you are already caring for her. She has an uncle already settled in Oregon and we need only see her safely to him."

"What did you tell him?"

"I said—yes."

She nodded. "Of course we will take care of her. I'll go and tell her."

"Also," Edgar continued, "there is the matter of her family's wagon. We are to search it and remove what money and valuables we can find, and save them for her. And what foodstuffs and other things we need to accommodate her. Then, everyone else will be allowed to examine what is left and buy items. We are to save this money for Catherine. What remains will be abandoned for those behind us to use what they can." Gertie listened quietly as the child cried quietly in her lap. It sounded so cruel and yet was necessary.

They found a little more than a hundred dollars; Gertie was careful to examine all the trunks for false bottoms. They kept this and most of the food. An additional amount of fifty dollars was collected from those who purchased items from the wagon. The items were worth much more than they collected, but no one had money to spare.

The next morning, the wagon train once again set off. However, the misery of the trail had become oppressive. There was no game and they were forced to eat their remaining dried meat. Gertie reminisced about all the misery she had faced since arriving in Independence, Missouri. Each hardship had hardened her in preparation for the next one. Each new tribulation was a greater trial than those before it.

Oh, Lord, what can possibly lie ahead, she prayed. As she had done day after day, she put the rising sun to her back and began walking westward.

Several days later, they abandoned the shallow trickling stream which was all that remained of the Sweetwater River. Its headwaters were in the mountains to the north, but they continued west. Once again, everyone was instructed to fill all their water barrels to the brim, designating the water for the oxen teams. This chore took quite some time as individuals formed a bucket brigade from the thin flow of water to the barrels. The wagon train angled to the southwest and they continued their march over gentle slopes of barren hills. At midday, it appeared as though they were spending more time going downhill than up.

"This is it? This is the South Pass?" Gertie asked in amazement.

The wagon train had stopped for their noon meal and the Merry Widows busied themselves cooking. Gertie had been expecting the infamous path through the mountains would be a dramatic canyon with a hidden entrance and sheer rock walls. However, this place was a wide open space with gentle hills leading to a low mountain in the north. There was nothing but sand to the south.

"Yes, that is what Major Jamison says," Beth announced. "This is the South Pass. All the rivers—the Sweetwater and Platte Rivers—to the east flow into the Atlantic Ocean. All the streams and rivers we encounter going forward will be flowing into the Pacific Ocean."

"It's true," Mrs. Clark agreed. "We are now in Oregon Territory." She chuckled. "But still far from our destination."

Gertie snorted a short laugh. "I expected so much more. All this time we have been striving to reach the South Pass, and here it is—a mere patch of sandy hill." Sweat dripped from her nose and she wiped her face. She had no idea what the temperature might be, but she could not recall ever being so hot. "At least there are no darn mosquitoes here." She mimicked swatting and scratching.

The three widows and the orphaned girl laughed. Gertie noted this was the first time Catherine had laughed since the death of her father.

By the end of the day, an oasis of green grass and low shrubs opened before them. The sharp contrast with the surrounding sand and olive sagebrush could be seen a mile away. Drawing closer, they found a stream. Meager as it was, they turned south and followed it in the direction of its flow.

"This," Major Jamison announced, "is aptly named Pacific Springs. It is where we begin to follow the water to the Pacific Ocean."

For two and a half months Gertie had always been walking along rivers against the water's flow, now she was following the water. The water was now leading her to her future in Oregon. With renewed vigor, she quickstepped forward to walk beside Edgar. He was driving the oxen; however, they required no encouragement to pull the wagon down the hill to the water. She reached out and took his hand in hers. He kissed her and she dreamed of a future with him always by her side.

Two days later they crossed the Green River. The trek through the desert was finished. The river was teeming with trout and they fashioned nets from spare canvas. Scooping these into the water, they drew out countless fish for their first meal of fresh meat in several days. No one felt they had tasted better—ever! Their bellies and appetites were satisfied.

After this feast, it was two more days and they arrived at Fort Bridger.

* * *

Fort Bridger and into the mountains

"It doesn't look like much," Gertie stated to Edgar, as they watched the smudge on the horizon. It slowly grew in size as they plodded forward.

"Nope. Major Jamison says it was once a fur trapper's trading post, but now the Mormons have taken it over. Our Mormon friends are almost home. The Great Salt Lake is not too many miles over those mountains." Edgar pointed to the purple mounds on the horizon to the west.

Isn't that the way to California as well? She did not speak the words for fear it would alter his mood. She still feared that he would leave her for the distant gold fields.

"Which way are we going?" Gertie asked. She wanted clarification, but was unwilling to directly ask the question which plagued her.

"We are going to turn to the north and pass between those mountains," he pointed to a gap in the purple mounds on the horizon. "Not much but mountain after mountain ahead of us."

She breathed a sigh of relief; he had said 'we'. He was not going to abandon her.

Fort Bridger was as much of an anticlimax as had been South Pass. It was a wooden stockade half the size of Fort John. Gertie could see where mud had been packed between the wood poles. The result left the building looking just slightly more civilized than the homes had been in the Pawnee village.

There were dozens of wagons camped around the fort, but their numbers were nothing like those that had been gathered at Fort John.

"We will stay for two days here," Major Jamison announced. "Anyone who needs supplies or repairs should get to it. The Mormons bring flour from their wheat fields here to sell. If you can afford it, stock up."

Gertie was glad Mrs. Clark did not suggest that they look for the saloon. She was certain the Mormons would not have allowed one to exist. Even if one existed, she had experienced all the saloon *entertainment* she needed for one lifetime.

When they once again yoked their oxen and snapped the whip to continue their journey westward, Gertie could wait no longer. She required an answer to her question. It was the question which triggered the doubt that consumed most of her waking hours.

Am I going to be a part of his life? she asked herself. And then said aloud, "Edgar, what of California? Are you still thinking of that as your destination?"

He smiled.

"Oh, yes, my love. I still think I am better suited as a merchant in the gold fields than a farmer in the Willamette Valley. However, this looks to be a good direction to go today. We have Catherine to consider. We must see her to her uncle's home. Then we'll have a look at Oregon before deciding what to do next."

"We-we are going to decide?"

"Yes, I think it is something we should decide together."

Her eyes welled up with tears of happiness, and warmth enveloped her soul. While not exactly a proposal of marriage, she was very comforted to know Edgar was not going to abandon her. The anxiety she had been feeling faded away.

As the wagon train passed between the tall green mountains, water, grass, and game were once again plentiful.

"Now this is what I imagined South Pass to look like," Gertie remarked to her friends. They were camped in a rich green valley with shear mountainsides to the west and east. They were traveling north, following the Bear River. There were no buffalo in the mountains, and few deer. However, there was a significant population of mountain goats. Edgar hunted these fine tasting animals. After a few days of climbing steep rocky slopes passing from one mountain to another, sometimes advancing no more than a hand full of miles, they were once again traversing green grassy valleys.

When they reached the Portneuf River they were noticeably heading downhill. The days passed quickly and the change from desert terrain was a blessing. The time flew by as they walked through the beautiful mountains. One day, the valley opened wide and they descended onto a huge plain. The fields of grass stretched for miles to the north, east, and west. Remembering the bleakness of the desert, Gertie thought she was in heaven.

"Where are we," she asked of Edgar.

"That is the Snake River and Fort Hall up ahead. I was here two days ago scouting out the place. You won't like it any better than Fort Bridger, except it is not run by Mormons."

They camped at Fort Hall for two days to allow their animals to graze and regain strength. Some of the oxen were too weak to continue and these were traded for fresh animals. The weakened oxen would be fattened and traded to travelers behind them. Unfortunately the trading post offered little in the way of other food and supplies.

Edgar hunted the buffalo roaming the valley and was able to refill their supply of raw meat for drying. "Major Jamison says the dry land ahead will have little game," he said. Gertie was pleased to cut the meat and hang it on the drying frame she kept in the wagon. As she worked, she noticed the boys tossing something back and forth. Looking closer she noticed they were throwing the flat dried buffalo turds. Children would find games with anything anywhere, she smiled and mused to herself.

* * *

The Snake River

When their westward journey resumed, they followed the twists and turns of the appropriately named Snake River. For a time it was as though they were back on the grassy plains. Even the Indians reappeared. However, these natives watched the emigrants from a distance and made no attempt to assist them during the river crossings. Major Jamison ordered the wagons to camp close together during the nights in an effort to thwart any attempt that the Indians might make to steal the livestock. They had been warned at Fort Hall that these Snake Indians were not friendly.

A week after leaving Fort Hall, they entered an area of widespread black lava flows. The life giving waters of the river plunged over an enormous waterfall into a deep canyon. The sheer walls of this gorge precluded any attempt at retrieving drinking water. The river at the bottom of the gorge tantalized them—so close, but so unreachable.

Without the river's water, the land turned to desert as they made their way from waterhole to waterhole. Gertie found this stretch of wretched land to be unbearable. The months of the never ending cycle of breaking camp in the morning, walking for eight to ten hours, and then cooking and camping once more had taken all the reserve from her. Were it not for the encouraging talks given by Major Jamison each evening, and his barking commands each morning, she would have stopped dead in her tracks.

Each day they passed exhausted emigrants who had stopped alongside the trail.

"Hurry along," Major Jamison attempted to encourage the stragglers, "winter will be upon us all too soon. The mountains ahead cannot be crossed after the snow falls."

Without question, these stragglers were welcomed to join the wagon train. Some had stopped not due to a lack of will, but because their wagons had broken down or their oxen had died. Some had been attacked by Indians. With their own collection of spare parts and extra animals exhausted, Major Jamison could not set these unfortunate soles right. They had no choice but to abandon their belongings and join the wagon train with only that which they could carry. Major Jamison accepted what food they had as payment for joining.

One of these stragglers was William Chapman. "He's from Tennessee," Beth said. She had taken an instant liking to him. "He was traveling with a group of wagons, but his wheel broke. They had no spare and his companions set off to find a wheel and bring it back to him. However, after three days they have not returned and he thinks they abandoned him."

"That is a rather deplorable way to treat a friend," Gertie responded.

"I gather they weren't exactly friends. He says, there has been nothing but strife among them for the past month. Anyway, I've offered to take what manner of his possessions that my wagon will hold."

"I see," Gertie said with a knowing smile. She surmised Beth was taking some of Grace's advice and seeking a man to marry.

With the pathway more downhill than up, the land eventually dropped. The tall sides of the gorge surrounding the river diminished until they were once again alongside the Snake River. They fed on the fish which filled the river.

After another week, they were back in the mountains. The land surrounding the Snake River canyon was too rugged to allow the wagons to continue following the river. While the Snake River turned north, they continued a westerly direction following the Grande Rondo River, into the mountains.

"Where does it go?" Gertie asked of Major Jamison, pointing to the Snake River.

"It winds through a sheer canyon ahead, but eventually empties into the Columbia River less than fifty miles upstream of where we are going, Umatilla Landing. We are nearing the end of our journey," he continued. "Less than fifty miles over these hills is Waiilatpu and the Whitman Mission."

The Major valiantly tried to lift the spirits of the weary emigrants. Their food supplies were long gone and the malnourished travelers were surviving on meat alone. Fortunately, game was still plentiful. The Powder River valley was the most handsome land she had seen since leaving Bear River. The valley was several miles wide, covered with a heavy coat of grass. To the west loomed the high range of the Blue Mountains. The whole country abounded with deer and prairie chickens.

Most of the women adopted Gertie's practice of driving the ox team while the men hunted. Gertie marveled at how tame the oxen had become. After pulling the wagon day after day for so long, the beasts thought of nothing else. With nothing more than a verbal command, they would strain with all their remaining strength to haul the wagon up the steep hills. In the morning, when the train set into motion, her oxen would begin the day's journey as soon as the wagon in front of them began to move. Her oxen required no instructions from her at all.

What a blessing, she mused for she had no energy left to whip them.

With all of their provisions gone, the wagons had room for the settlers to sleep inside. Everyone abandoned the ritual of setting up tents. Other than frying the meat, they abandoned cooking as well.

While traversing the Blue Mountains, the wagon train was overtaken by a small band of Indians. Fearing the worst, the wagons closed in together as best they could in the narrow canyon. Gertie watched as Edgar checked the load in his Hawken, rifle and joined Major Jamison and his scouts to meet the intruders.

"I am Five Crows, Chief of the Cayuse, Dr. Whitman's Indians," their leader said.

Everyone sighed with relief. They all knew of Marcus Whitman and his wife Narcissa. They had been among the earliest settlers in the Oregon Territory and operated a mission to help other immigrants and the local Indians.

Five Crows spoke nearly perfect English and was the finest looking Indian Gertie had seen. He was of a medium height with muscular limbs. He was dressed in a buckskin pants like Edgar had been wearing when she had met him; however, he wore a calico shirt sown from several patches of cloth. Unlike any other Indian, he wore short hair under a broad brimmed hat. Were it not for his bronze skin, she would not have known he was an Indian.

"What is happening?" Gertie asked Edgar when he returned from the meeting.

"He seems to be a rather fine fellow. He claims to be a Christian. They are a hunting party and have offered us meat and potatoes."

"Goodness, I would dearly love a potato!"

The Indians remained with the wagons. They rode their ponies along the length of the train peering into each wagon. Nervous that the Indians were plotting to steal from them, the emigrants kept their weapons handy. That evening, the Indians did not camp by themselves, but rather they mingled among the wagons.

"May I dine with you?" Five Crows asked of Edgar. They were eating the food the Indians had provided, so Edgar welcomed the man to join them. "You are Mormon? These women are your wives?" he asked, observing Gertie, Beth, and Grace together. "These are your daughters?" He pointed toward Catherine and Marjorie.

"No, these women are widows. Their husbands died along the way here and I am taking care of them." Edgar observed a change in Five Crows expression, and he added, "I am seeing them safely to the Willamette Valley."

"Ah," Five Crows answered.

"Your English is excellent," Edgar observed.

"Ah, yes, Dr. Whitman has a school and invites everyone to attend. There are many among the Cayuse and Umatilla peoples who speak English." The Indian slowly extended his hand to touch Beth's red hair. "I've never seen such beautiful hair."

"She's with me." William Chapman said, walking into the camp. He touched Five Crows' hand and he withdrew it.

"Ah, she is lovely," the Indian said, and broadly smiled. "Such startling green eyes I've never seen before."

As they were preparing for bed, Edgar whispered to Gertie, "I want you and Catherine to sleep in the wagon. Mr. Chapman and I will sleep outside. We'll take turns watching over our new friends."

The emigrants were nervous with the Indians sleeping in their camp, but they exhibited no sign of thievery. In the morning, they offered their horses to assist the exhausted oxen in the effort to pull the wagons over the Blue Mountains.

This last leg of the journey proved to be the most difficult. Nine yoke of oxen and horses were hitched to one wagon to pull it up the steep mountainsides. Ropes and pulleys were used to lower the wagons down the opposite side. In this manner, the wagons were moved one by one. Once again, Gertie was pleased with Peter's insistence that they travel light with a small wagon. That night they camped, still within sight of where they had spent the previous night. After the day's labor, the Indians departed with a promise that they would return with more food.

High in the mountains, the nights were freezing cold. They had been traveling through the summer and did not have any winter clothing. Gertie, Edgar, and Catherine snuggled together under Edgar's buffalo hide. They slept much better than many others who had nothing except one or two blankets to keep them warm. The challenges of mountain travel continued and the cold began to sneak into their very bones. Gertie began to wish this part of the trek would end—soon. However, it took a full week for the wagon train to reach the plains on the northwestern slope of the mountains. The relief Gertie and Catherine felt was mirrored in the faces of the others. Thankfully, another leg of the journey was safely completed.

CHAPTER FOURTEEN

September 16, 1848
Whitman Mission

"Oh, my word the Lord is testing me." Gertie groaned to Edgar. The two sat in the wagon box as they surveyed the parched brown rolling hills of Oregon Territory which lay before them. After enjoying the beauty of rich green pine trees in the mountains, she was depressed by the sight, once again, of a brown desolate landscape. "I've not seen a patch of worthwhile land since we left the Kaw River. Why we did not stop there is beyond me."

He sighed, and agreed, "Indeed, this is not quite the heaven-on-earth we expected."

Gertie quickly decided to end her complaints; they would do nothing to alleviate their situation.

"Fear not," Mr. Woodstock said as he rode by, "this is simply another test for you. The green meadows you were promised are a mere two hundred miles east, along the Columbia River. You'll be there in two weeks." He clicked his tongue and his horse picked up the pace. "The Major is calling one last meeting tonight," he said over his shoulder.

As the weary travelers descended into the Columbia River valley, their journey with the wagon train was officially finished. Umatilla Landing on the Columbia River was a single, long day's ride ahead. There, barges on the river stopped to gather cargo brought over the trail. This post was the end of the line for Major Jamison and the merchants who had been hauling cargo. However, the pathway along the river to Oregon City and the Willamette Valley was well marked and dotted with settlements. Thus, the new settlers were on their own in this tame and safely traveled land.

With the sun low in the west, they camped beside the Umatilla River, a quarter mile from a small Indian village. These Umatilla Indians lived in small log houses as did the American settlers. Being friendly and English speaking, the Indians joined them and traded fresh meat and vegetables for whatever items the emigrants had left. Nearing the end of their trek, many of Gertie's companions traded away their blankets, extra canvas, anything they imagined they could survive without in exchange for the food. Gertie was willing to part with most anything to fill her belly.

"To give you an idea of what's ahead for you," the Major began at the nightly meeting, "from here, you will continue west to what is known as The Dalles. The trail is well marked and you won't have any problem following it. You are all experienced with making river crossings, so if you stay together and assist one another, you will have no trouble. At The Dalles, you will have to remove your wagon wheels and load the wagons on barges. You will have to pay for this passage, unless you choose to build your own rafts. There is no roadway through the steep walls of the gorge, but there is a narrow footpath. Someone in your group will have to walk your livestock, in single file, along this way. When you get to the Cascade Rapids, you will have to reassemble your wagons and wait for your livestock to join you. Then take the narrow road around the rapids. Once again, you will have to remove the wheels and load everything onto a boat which will take you to the Willamette River and to Oregon City. That is it, you will have finally arrived at the land you were promised. It does exist, it is really there."

The crowd began to converse among themselves and the Major had to shout his next words to regain their attention. "However, there is another way, he continued. "Once you reach The Dalles, you can follow the Barlow Road. This is a land path which you can follow to take your wagons around Mount Hood directly to the Oregon City." He paused to gesture toward the giant mountain to the west. This will take a bit longer, and it is a difficult path. There is a toll for using this road, but it is cheaper than the cost of the barges on the river."

"Which means do you recommend?" someone asked.

"We have arrived at least a month before bad weather. The land path will remain passable until it snows. It takes longer, but all things considered, I would take this road to the Willamette Valley."

The people again murmured forcing the Wagon master to shout his final words, "You don't have to make the decision until you reach The Dalles. The water route is faster, but more expensive and frequently more dangerous than the land route."

That night Catherine slept in a tent while Edgar and Gertie made love inside the nearly empty wagon. When they had finished, he began to whisper to her.

"Darling, I think it is time we talked about the future."

"Yes," she whispered back, thinking it was definitely time they talked about the future.

"I know only men can claim the promised 320 acres in the Willamette Valley. And if that is what you want, then I will continue there with you and make this claim." He paused to take a breath and hugged her closely to him. "But you know it is not my desire to be a farmer. If you want the land, I will stay with you to build a homestead—"

"No," she interrupted. "That is not what I want. I want to go to California... with you. I want to be where you are." The homestead in Oregon had been Peter's dream. Gertie didn't care where she ended up; she simply wanted to live with Edgar.

Edgar hugged her again and she sensed his smile in the darkness. He kissed her tenderly.

"I'm very happy to hear you say that. In this case, I hope you will consent to becoming my wife as soon as we can find a preacher."

Gertie had read many engagement scenes in romance books and she had always imagined this is what it would be like for her—her fiancé dropping to one knee while begging for her hand. She had been robbed of this experience with her parents' introduction of Peter—she had been commanded to marry him. He had not asked for her hand. Once again, it seemed this romantic, fictional image was not for her. She concluded this image was only for the stories—it was fiction.

"Yes," she sighed. "That is exactly what I want, as well. It is my dream come true." She was to be Edgar's wife. For better or for worse, for richer or for poorer— for the rest of her life. Her heart soared with radiant joy. For the first time in her life, she knew what love really was.

"Good, my love," Edgar said. "I discussed this with Major Jamison, and there is a third means of getting down the river. I suggest we follow the Major to the Umatilla Landing. There we can divest ourselves of this wagon and take the minimum possible amount of our belongings on a cargo boat down the Columbia River to the port city. There we can get passage on a ship to San Francisco. We no longer need this wagon or any of this and there is no need to continue carrying it along."

"I want to keep my trunk," she stated. She knew what Edgar considered packing light to be, and that would be a far cry less than what Peter had allowed her.

He paused for a moment, and then agreed. "I believe we can pack all of what we need in your trunk. We can carry it with us in the boat."

"But, Edgar, what of Catherine?"

"Once we get to Oregon City, we can rent a room. From there, we will find her uncle and take Catherine to her family. Then we will continue on our sea voyage."

Comforted that there was a plan for the young girl's future, Gertie snuggled beside Edgar and fell asleep.

The following morning, most of their friends pulled up stakes and continued toward The Dalles. Olga had grown to consider her traveling companions to be more than friends. After the grueling trek, they had become family. There were many tearful goodbyes as she feared she would never see them again. Before heading downriver to the Umatilla Landing, the Major exchanged handshakes with all the men and his wife exchanged hugs with all the women.

Edgar, the three widows, William Chapman, and the two girls chose to remain in camp and gather their strength. Late in the morning rain poured down and the small party sought refuge in a lodge near the center of the Indian village.

The owner of the lodge, an Indian called Stickas, greeted them and served them hot tea. They had exhausted their supply of coffee weeks earlier and Gertie was in heaven sipping this warm brew.

"Why are you not making way to The Dalles," Stickas asked Edgar.

"It is our intention to sell our rigs and ride down the Columbia River in a boat," Edgar answered, speaking for the group. "Do you know who might buy our wagons?"

"No, there are many settlers around who might want them, but few have any money."

In the early afternoon the rain abated and two men arrived riding upstream beside the Umatilla River. One rode in a buckboard wagon drawn by two horses while the other rode on horseback. They both wore oiled canvas wrapped around themselves to ward off the remains of the rain.

"Dr. Whitman, I've been expecting you." Stickas greeted the horseback rider.

"Indeed, we are late," he replied. "We paused to preach the Sabbath service in Umatilla, and then were delayed by the rain." The doctor turned toward the band of emigrants. He smiled and Gertie imagined he found their dirty, ragged appearance comical. Dusty and sunburned, they looked more like the Indians than Americans. "Hello," he said, extending his hand to Edgar, "I am Dr. Marcus Whitman. I presume that you were in Major Jamison's party." Not pausing for an answer, he continued, "Ah, indeed, Chief Five Crows told me of your arrival."

"It is a pleasure to make your acquaintance, sir. I am Edgar Millar." Edgar completed the introductions for Gertie and the others, and Dr. Whitman introduced his companion, Joseph Stanfield.

With the arrival of Dr. Whitman, Stickas produced a spread of meat and vegetables for the midday meal. Edgar, Gertie, and the others were invited to join. However, as the meal had clearly been intended for the three men, there was insufficient food. Thus, the emigrants feigned that they had already eaten and watched the others feast.

As they ate, Stickas reported that the measles epidemic was once again among the Indians. And if the sickness itself wasn't bad enough he went on to say, "There is a half breed from Maine by the name of Jo Lewis who is making trouble," he added. "He is telling our people that you and Mr. Spaulding are poisoning the

Indians so as to give their country to your own people." He glanced sheepishly toward Gertie and the others. "Of course, I know this not to be true, but many others believe him."

Marcus Whitman silently mulled the information. Speaking to no one in particular, he said, "Have any of you already been sick with the measles? It is known that you cannot contract it twice and we could use several more hands to help us tend to the sick at our mission."

After some discussion they learned Beth and Catherine had also been afflicted, but Edgar, William, Grace, and Marjorie had not. "I've already had it," Gertie announced. "I'd be happy to help you." Beth and Catherine nodded in agreement.

"Splendid," Marcus stated, "we shall be on our way at once and arrive by nightfall."

Edgar pulled Gertie aside and whispered to her, "Please, don't' go. We don't know these people." Gertie returned a scowl, and Edgar elaborated, "I'm not saying Dr. Whitman is a threat, but we know," he nodded his head toward Stickas, "that the Indians are upset with the emigrants. This is not a good idea."

"These Indians have been very good to us. I dare say some of our party might have perished in the Blue Mountains had it not been for the aid from Chief Five Crows. I believe we owe them what help we can give. It is our Christian duty."

Edgar's jaw twitched, but he found no effective argument to dissuade her.

Gertie kissed him goodbye and took her place next to Beth and Catherine in the buckboard wagon. She watched Edgar as they rode away. Being unable to dissuade her, he stood solemnly staring after them until they were out of sight.

It was after dark when they completed the 25 miles to the Whitman Mission. After travelling at the slow pace of the oxen for so long, Gertie marveled at the speed with which the horses pulled the small wagon. She tied her bonnet tightly under her chin to keep it from blowing away.

"This is my wife, Narcissa." Dr. Whitman introduced the large, well-formed woman of fair complexion. She had auburn hair a nose slightly too large for her face, and soft gray eyes. She in turn introduced Perrin, Dr. Whitman's nephew, Mary Ann Badger, and David Cortez. These last two were nine and seven year old children adopted by the Whitmans.

Narcissa ushered her husband up the stairs to the sick room while a young, but mature for her age, Mary Ann toured them through the mission house. After so many months along the Trail, Gertie found the warm fireplace, stuffed chairs, genuine cooking stove, and enclosed privy to be unbelievable luxuries. Mary Ann explained she and David were half Indian who spoke fluently in both the Cayuse and English languages. She warmed some food for the weary travelers. Following their light meal of cornbread and beans, the women went to the upstairs sickroom to relieve Dr. and Mrs. Whitman in the tending of the sick children. The stench of sickness almost overwhelmed them when they entered the room. The children lay upon cots or on blanket pallets on the floor. Most were quiet, but some moaned softly. Gertie immediately began to minister to the nearest child. The little girl appeared to be about five. She was covered in the rash of the disease and burned with a fever whhich frightened Gertie. Water in a wash basin contained a cloth which Gertie wrung out and began to wipe the fevered brow of the child.

Without rest, they attended the stricken children through the night. One Indian child died, but most of the others had improved by morning. They wouldn't be able to tell for sure for a day or two, but it seemed as if the worst of the disease had run its course.

With the rising sun, Gertie went downstairs and stepped outside for some fresh air. It was a cold, foggy morning, but she could see the expanse of the mission grounds. She admired the cows as they munched the bright green grass of the pasture bordered by dark green trees. As she had read in the pamphlets, Oregon was indeed a slice of heaven on earth.

This is the Oregon I was promised.

Mary Ann prepared breakfast, but most everyone was either too tired or too sick to eat.

Dr. Whitman carried the body of the dead Indian child outside, and Gertie followed for a short distance. She watched the brief burial service in the graveyard. Looking around, she watched men operate the grist mill. Between the Mission House and the Mill, Mr. Stanfield was butchering a cow beside another house. A large number of Indians were gathered under the trees beside the millpond.

"There is trouble here," Beth spoke softly beside her. "There is a sense of tension and danger hanging about the place and I cannot shake the feeling from my mind." Gertie's earlier feeling of joy at the beauty of Oregon had begun to dwindle at the time of the funeral. Something felt amiss to her as well. Gertie met Beth's eyes as she continued, "Edgar was right; we should not have come."

Dr. Whitman returned from the funeral and joined them in the main room. He began giving assignments for the various medicines to be taken up to the sickroom. Narcissa walked through to the kitchen to retrieve some milk.

After a few seconds, her exit to the kitchen was followed by her frightened scream.

Through the open door, Gertie saw several Indians surround Narcissa. As they advanced upon her, she spun on her heel and managed to flee back into the main room. As one boisterous Indian attempted to follow, Narcissa slammed the door in his face and bolted it. Immediately, the Indians began pounding on the door, demanding to speak with Dr. Whitman.

"I'll go and see what they want," he said, opening the door. "However, bolt the door behind me."

Narcissa bolted the door a second time. She and Gertie listened, but could not discern the conversation in the kitchen.

An explosive gunshot startled them. Stumbling backward, the two women fell to the floor. Leaping up, Narcissa ordered the children upstairs.

"Oh, the Indians! The Indians have killed my husband!" she cried to Gertie.

Mary Ann had been in the kitchen, cleaning. However, at the beginning of the violence she had fled outdoors. Having run around the outside of the house, she entered the main room.

"What has happened?" Gertie asked the deathly white young girl.

"Father is dead," she blurted out.

Several emigrants followed Mary Ann through the door into the main room.

Narcissa locked the outside door. Hearing nothing from the adjoining kitchen, she unbolted the door. Finding the room devoid of Indians, she and Gertie brought Marcus' body into the main room. Sobbing, Narcissa whispered, "Oh my dear husband, you are dead and I am now a widow. Why, oh why?"

Gaining control of her grief, Narcissa pulled herself to her feet and looked out the window. She exclaimed at what she saw, "It's that wretched Jo Lewis. He is doing it all." She pointed to an Indian running across the grounds, chasing down a screaming emigrant.

With a nearly constant roar of gunfire, the women watched helplessly as Indians murdered the emigrants camped around the mission. One man, running from his attackers, rushed to the door and Narcissa let him inside. He had a broken arm and a deep gash in his scalp.

"Mrs. Whitman, the Indians are killing us all!" he shouted.

A bullet flew through the window and struck Narcissa in the shoulder. Clasping her wound, she shrieked in pain. As she fell to the floor, Gertie tried to help her up.

"Save yourselves," she said to Gertie. "Get to the children upstairs. Lord, save the little ones," she prayed.

The wounded man pushed the women to the stairway. He handed a small child to Gertie. Holding it tightly in her arms, she ran up the stairs. Jo Lewis broke down the door and fired a volley of gunshots, killing Narcissa and the wounded man. With a fleeting look back at the carnage, Gertie continued up the stairs to the sick room above.

Gertie hid in the upstairs room with the women and children. They listened as the Indians ransacked the lower rooms. Taking control of the lower level, their presence imprisoned the women in the upper room. The Indians did not attempt to climb the stairs. Gertie reasoned they were afraid of catching the sickness from the children.

Darkness fell and the cries of the wounded abated as they died. It was a long night of fear and horror as the women and children tried to remain quiet. When morning arrived, the Christian Indians gained permission from Jo Lewis to bury the dead.

CHAPTER FIFTEEN

September 17, 1848
Captivity

Without food or water Gertie and the others huddled together. Through the windows, they watched the Indians carry away the bodies. The terrifying sounds of the Indians in the house below continued hour after hour. The time passed with agonizing slowness. Hearing footsteps climbing the stairs, Gertie mentally prepared for death. Holding her breath, she awaited what fate had in store of each of them.

Please, dear God, let death come quickly!

The door at the top of the stairs opened and several of the fearsome Indians appeared. One appeared to be part white and Gertie recognized him to be the Indian identified by Narcissa as Jo Lewis. He spoke several sentences in the Cayuse native tongue and Mary Ann interpreted.

"He says we will not be hurt. He is going to take us to Fort Walla Walla." She held her lips close to Gertie's ear and whispered, "But he is lying. I heard them talking earlier, and they have nothing but treachery on their minds."

Nonetheless, Gertie nodded agreement to Jo Lewis and he left, leaving three Indians behind. One of these spoke and Mary Ann again interpreted, "They want you two," she motioned to Gertie and Beth, "to go downstairs. They say there is food there for you to cook and feed everyone." She swallowed hard. "They say Dr. Whitman's poison has killed their wives and now you must be their wives. The one speaking is Tamsucky. He is one of the worst of the Indians and you should not make him angry."

Compassion won out over fear. Unable to endure the cries of the sick, hungry, thirsty children any longer, Gertie tugged on Beth's sleeve. "Let's go," she said. "We must save the children. What else can they do to us?" Fearful that she knew exactly what evil they could perpetrate upon them, she held Beth's hand and followed Tamsucky into the kitchen.

The lower rooms were an indiscriminate mass of broken furniture, feathers, ash, straw, blood, and God knew what else. Gertie and Beth gasped, and pushed as much of the debris as they could out of the kitchen.

The Indians did not interfere as the two women prepared the meal. Gertie suspected they were afraid that the food had been poisoned when they insisted the children eat first. However, she was grateful for the opportunity to give them a full measure of food before the Indians devoured it.

After Gertie and Beth cleaned the kitchen, they spread mattresses on the floor of the main room. The Indians took possession of the beds, but would not allow the two women to return to the upstairs room. Lying in the warmth beside the stove, they sought sleep. In the middle of the night, Beth kicked Gertie to awaken her. Springing up, she saw Tamsucky hovering over Beth. His hands savagely fondled her body and pushed up her skirt.

"No-NO!" Beth shouted, as she struggled to free herself from his grasp.

Gertie lashed out with her leg and kicked him in the stomach. He released Beth and swung a fist toward Gertie. Twisting away, she protected her face, and took the blow on her shoulder. Beth took advantage of the moment to slip past him. She ran outside screaming for help.

Tamsucky pursued her.

The other two Indians were awakened by the struggle and they held Gertie, preventing her from further assisting her friend. Tamsucky put his hand over Beth's mouth to squelch her screams and tried to throw her across his pony. Beth climbed up and over the horse. Tumbling to the ground, she slipped free. As she ran screaming for help, Tamsucky regained his hold upon her and wrestled her to the ground. Gertie watched helplessly as the Indian had his way with her. When he finished, he carried the sobbing disheveled Beth back to the house and released her. Gertie helped the abused and stunned young woman up the stairs and held her until she fell asleep.

In the morning, Chief Five Crows arrived.

"Oh! You Fools!" he shouted at the other Indians, "Has the coyote stolen your brains? You have killed the best friends the Indians will ever have. This will bring a war with the American man. Heed my words."

After sending Tamsucky away, he spoke to Beth, "You must come with me. Tamsucky intends to have you for his wife, but I can protect you if you come and live in my lodge."

Beth began to softly cry. "What should I do?" she asked of Gertie.

"Chief Five Crows has not deceived us. He has been kind and never displayed any reason to distrust him."

Beth reluctantly agreed to leave the Mission with Five Crows. Pretending to take her captive, he bound her wrists and tied her to a pony before leading her away.

With extreme sadness in her heart, Gertie prayed she would see her friend once again.

Throughout the horrific day, Gertie and Catherine did their best to follow the treatment plan laid out by Dr. Whitman as they cared for the sick children. The Indians did not interfere with the two women's nursing tasks and by the end of the next day the children were well on the road to recovery. Their fevers had broken; none had died during the night. Some were even sitting up and attempting to play the games of children. They showed remarkable resilience in their recovery from the deadly disease. Gertie, however, could not help but think of the child Dr. Whitman had buried at the edge of the yard and those who had died prior to their arrival.

The evening meal had to be prepared to feed the children and the Indians who remained in the building. Jo Lewis was nowhere to be seen and Gertie wondered what had become of him. Exhausted, Gertie, Catherine, and Mary Ann cleaned up the remains of the evening meal. This was when Tamsucky returned.

"He says his wife has died and he insists that he have the red-haired woman," Mary Ann interpreted. "He means Mrs. Howe," she needlessly added.

Gertie knew that, like Chief Five Crows, Tamsucky had been smitten by Beth's glorious red hair.

Tamsucky searched the house. Not finding Beth, he grabbed Gertie and forced her into the main room. She ran for the door, but two Indians blocked her path and pushed her into a chair. Tamsucky began talking in his native tongue, but Gertie needed no interpretation to understand his nefarious meaning. She knew exactly what he meant.

"Go upstairs with the others," she told Mary Ann and Catherine. Gertie saw no reason for the children to witness what the evil she Tamsucky intended to do to her.

The other two Indians watched as Tamsucky was surprisingly gentle with her. He danced for her; he spoke softly to her. She was reminded of the mating dance the Pawnee had performed the day Edgar had taken her to the Indian village, and recognized that Tamsucky was courting her. Despite his best efforts to charm her into submission, she continued to refuse him. Following Edgar's advice from months ago, she steeled her face and displayed no fear to the Indians.

"Get away from me!" She slapped his hands away every time he touched her. Tamsucky eventually tired of the contest. Gathering her hands in one of his, he brutally pinned her wrists behind her back and used his free hand to grope her breasts through her clothing. He reached for the hem of her skirt.

Kicking and screaming, Gertie fought with him as best she could, but her actions merely assisted him as he pulled her skirt up to expose her legs.

He growled unintelligible words from deep within his throat.

Jerking her up from the chair, he threw her to the ground. He unwound a strip of leather from around his waist. He snapped it like a whip. With all gentleness gone, he thrashed the backs of her legs. Gertie screamed for the other Indians to help, but they would not interfere.

Whimpering in agony, Gertie stopped her struggles and lay silent.

Tamsucky rolled her onto her back. Standing over her, he opened his trousers and expose his manhood. Gertie kicked her leg up. Enough was enough, she had no intention of remaining the helpless victim. With all her might, she drove her shoe squarely into his crotch.

The Indian's face instantly morphed into a ghoulish silent scream. His eyes rolled back and he collapsed. Struggling to breathe, his body shook with the pain.

The other two Indians broke into laughter. One stood beside Gertie, holding her down, while the other bent over Tamsucky in an attempt console him.

A fourth Indian entered through the door, but he showed no interest in the proceedings. While taller than the other Indians, he was hunched over with a blanket covering his head and shoulders. Limping like an old man, he walked to the fireplace and began to warm himself. After a moment, the Indian standing beside Gertie approached him. The newcomer ignored the Indian when he spoke.

Abruptly, the tall man tossed off the blanket and Gertie saw the flashing glimmer of polished steel as he thrust a knife into the gut of the surprised Indian.

"*Edgar!*" she cried out. She instantly recognized her lover dressed in his buckskin suit.

Withdrawing his Bowie knife, Edgar's eyes briefly met hers. He grinned.

As the Indian crouching beside Tamsucky stood, Edgar lunged and drove the big knife deep into the center of his chest. Edgar paused for a moment. With a look of savagery, he bent over Tamsucky. Edgar was an avenging angel who, with one quick slash, slit Tamsucky's throat. Avoiding the spray of blood, Gertie's rescuer wiped the blade of the big knife clean on Tamsucky's shirt. The calm yet intensely aware Edgar turned to Gertie.

"Are you all right?" he asked.

"Yes-yes, I'm fine. They didn't hurt me." She assumed it was not the whipping which troubled him most.

He lifted her face to his and tenderly kissed her lips.

"Are you sure?" His concerned eyes peered deeply into hers.

"They didn't hurt me," she repeated. She kissed him again, more deeply.

He wrapped her in his blanket and scooped her up in his strong arms. As he carried her to the door, Gertie complained, "The children, we can't leave them."

"They'll be fine. We'll be back before more Indians arrive. I promise," he said, and rushed out the doorway.

Holding her close, Edgar ran across the grassy meadow to the fence line. Several Indians spotted them and began to chase them. Upon reaching the fence, several Americans leapt up. Gertie recognized William Chapman and Joseph Stanfield among them. Aiming their rifles, the men began firing at the Indians.

"Stay here." Edgar gently lowered her to the ground. Taking up his Hawken rifle, he fired into the mêlée of Indians.

Not bothering to reload the rifle, Edgar drew his revolver and joined the charge of the other men. The shouting, cursing, gunshots were reminiscent of the Indian's original attack. However, this time the Americans held control as they chased the remaining Indians towards the mill pond. With the pond behind them, the Indians were trapped. A few continued to fight to the death. However, after just a few minutes of chaos and bloodshed, the outnumbered Indians surrendered.

As the fighting subsided, Gertie pulled the blanket tight around her shoulders and walked back to the Mission House. Mr. Chapman ran to join her, but Gertie blocked him from entering the house.

"She's not here," she said. As the color drained from his face, she realized she had left the impression that she was dead. "She's not hurt," Gertie clarified. "Chief Five Crows took her to his lodge to protect her." She swallowed. "But I don't know where that is." He spun around as though he could discern the direction himself. "I'm sure she is safe," Gertie reassured him.

As dawn broke, Gertie and Mary Ann helped them sort out which Indians were the actual perpetrators, and which had not participated in the massacre.

"How did you know to come save us?" she asked Edgar.

"One of the men working for Dr. Whitman hid under the floor of his house during the fighting, and escaped after dark. He ran through the night and the next morning to Umatilla. Henry Spaulding was his name. He reported what had happened; he knew nothing of your fate. However, several men gathered and we dashed here as quickly as we could. We arrived in the early evening, but waited until we could identify exactly where you and the other women and children were being held."

"Jo Lewis? What became of him?" Gertie asked. "He is a troublemaker, Edgar. We must be wary of his return. Oh, Edgar. I thought we were all going to die." Gertie could no longer hold the tears and they fell from her eyes to roll down her cheeks.

Edgar glanced away, as though searching for some answer in the distance. Turning back to Gertie, he embraced her. Dropping his voice to a whisper, he spoke of how he had affected her rescue. "I crept up to the building, with the intent of spying on them, but when I saw what the Indian did to you. I desperately wanted to help you, but had to wait until the time was right."

She hugged Edgar tighter.

"I'm all right. Other than the beating, he didn't hurt me."

"Yes, I saw." He chuckled. "I saw that you got the better of him." He held her tightly while they kissed. He stroked her hair. "I dare say," he continued, "that had you not rendered the one Indian helpless, I would not have been able to take all three at once."

Gertie looked away, not wanting to relive the brutal memory. "What are we going to do now?" she asked.

"They are going to take the Indians to Fort Walla Walla," he pointed toward the men guarding the bound Indians. "I guess you should go with them while Mr. Chapman and I search for Beth."

Gertie reluctantly agreed, but she did not want to be separated from him again. However, her concern was soon alleviated. Before Edgar and William Chapman could ready their mounts for the search, Chief Five Crows and Beth arrived.

"Ah, Mr. Millar, it is such a pleasure to see you once again." The Indian shook hands with Edgar, and helped Beth down from her pony. She ran into William's embrace

"My scouts told me of your battle with the coyote-brain Indians," Five Crows told Edgar. "I returned as quickly as I could."

Edgar told the chief of how they had retaken the Mission. "Now we are eager to return to the friends I left at the Umatilla landing I would appreciate the loan of your ponies and some assistance in hiring a boat from Umatilla to The Dalles."

The Chief laughed. "I would be honored to accompany you, but it is to Wallula that you should go. If it is a boat ride you intend to take, there is one at Walluha now which will be heading downriver soon. I will find you some ponies, and we can leave right away. That will be the fastest way to your friends at the Umatilla landing."

An hour later, the party mounted their horses. Catherine rode with Edgar on his stallion. Gertie, William, and Beth each rode ponies provided by the Indians. Five Crows, with two of his braves, directed their mounts west, along the Walla Walla River.

Riding side by side Gertie spoke quietly with Beth. "Are you all right? Did he treat you well?" she asked, nodding toward Five Crows.

Beth swallowed and composed her answer. "He wanted desperately to marry me. He became rather forceful at one point and I thought I had leapt from the frying pan into the fire. However, I told him I was promised to Mr. Chapman and eventually Five Crows relented." Beth sighed. "He didn't hurt me," she concluded.

Beth was glad they had made the correct choice. She said nothing of her own nearly disastrous fate.

After two hours of riding, they arrived at a small mission chapel.

"Is there a priest here?" Edgar asked the Indian Chief.

"Yes, his name is Father Broulliet."

"Let's stop here for a rest." Edgar dismounted and entered the chapel. While the others were dismounting, he returned with the priest. "Gertie," he said, "this is Father Broulliet and he has consented to marry us. I don't want another day to pass without you as my true wife."

Gertie leapt into his arms. "Oh yes, oh yes, I will," she said as tears welled in her eyes."I will marry you—now."

CHAPTER SIXTEEN

September 21, 1848
Wedding

The priest rang a bell and within half an hour several men and women settlers arrived. After exchanging a few words with them, the women set to work while the men took Edgar and William aside. One man supplied a bottle of whiskey for all to share.

"We are going to be married too," William proudly stated, hugging Beth to his side.

The two men congratulated each other as the women took Gertie and Beth into the chapel. A blanket had been strung up to create a partition. Gertie and Beth were escorted behind it. The local women decorated the two brides' hair with flower wreaths and placed veils over their heads. Lacking bridal gowns, they tied ribbons of blue and red to adorn their necks and waists. Their scuffed shoes were replaced with white slippers. Young Catherine's hair was also adorned with flowers; she would be each woman's bride's maid.

Though the trappings were simple, the prospect of a joyous wedding sparked a contagious excitement in the air. Gertie and Beth each felt to be a beautiful bride and even young Catherine glowed.

The bell was rung again, and the church door opened. Gertie heard the men folk enter the small chapel.

"What do I do first?" she heard William ask.

"Surely, get married," she heard Edgar answer with a chuckle.

The blanket was pulled aside and the two young women walked along the aisle to the altar.

Father Broulliet was dressed in his finest priestly robes and began the ceremony with passages from the Bible pertaining to marital advice. Gertie thought briefly of Peter and the life they might have had. Shame darkened her mind for a moment as she recalled taking these same vows with him, a mere six months earlier. She felt shame at being so happy with a different man. A man who she truly loved. She said a short prayer for Peter and closed the darkness from her mind. Smiling with the light heart of the girl inside every woman, she thought of the life that awaited her. She knew from experience Edgar would be kind and caring, and he would lovingly keep her safe all the days of her life.

When the vows began, she paid close attention and clearly articulated, "I do," at the appropriate time. This time, she really meant it.

"And now you may kiss the bride," Father Broulliet proclaimed.

Gertie turned toward her new husband. She tilted her face up and looked upon his chiseled face and smooth chin. She wondered when he had shaved as she pursed her lips. Edgar Millar lifted her veil and leaned down to bring their lips together. She closed her eyes.

She and her new husband kissed as though they had never kissed before. This touching of lips signified the deep and abiding love and the simmering passion they shared.

Stepping aside, they watched as the priest repeated the vows for Beth and William. After the second bride and groom kissed, they turned to smile at Gertie and Edgar. With the wedding ceremony completed, the witnesses and the newlyweds turned in mass and went outside. As though by magic, a spread of sweets and beverages had been assembled; the women had been busy. A violin provided music for the gathering.

For an hour, the Americans and Indians celebrated with food, laughter and dance. The two couples were so very much in love and so very happy. As they had many miles to go, time came for the merriment to end. The couples said their goodbyes and thanked everyone for all they had done. With a wave of their hands, smiles on their faces, and love in their hearts, the traveling party remounted their horses. The well-wishers shouted cheers as the newlyweds and their Indian companions rode away, continuing their trip to Wallula.

Arriving at Wallula, the two newlywed couples had no time for a proper honeymoon. Edgar thanked Chief Five Crows for his help. To show his deep appreciation and to Gertie's pleased surprise, Edgar gave his Hawken rifle to the Indian chief.

"Ah, thank you, Mr. Millar. I am the proudest Indian in Oregon to own such a fine rifle. I will kill many buffalo and provide meat for the winter for my tribe." The Indian Chief beamed.

That night, the women slept on tables in a small lodge while the men slept on the ground. In the morning, Edgar traded his horse for passage on a boat down the Columbia River. The forty-foot long, flat bottom Bateaux boat was loaded with furs and crewed by five Chinook Indians. When they stopped for the night at Umatilla Landing, Gertie greeted Grace and Marjorie, and collected her trunk.

Edgar and the Merry Widows are together once again, Gertie smiled.

"I sold everything as you directed," Grace said. She handed him a small purse partially full of coins. "While many people wanted to trade, few had any real money. Sadly, I mostly gave the stuff away."

"Mr. Millar," William Chapman said, "we are going to part company with you here. We are going to keep Beth's wagon and take it over the Barlow Road to the Willamette Valley. So, we will see you there."

"I don't believe we shall see one another in the Valley. You see, Gertie and I are continuing on to California by sailing ship after we find Catherine's family. We will have already left Oregon City by the time you arrive."

As quickly as the Merry Widows had reunited, they split apart. The widows' travels on the Oregon Trail had been long and grueling, but their friendship had grown. With deep sadness, the friends hugged each other and bid their final farewells. Gertie cried as the boat drifted away from the landing.

"I'm going to miss you!" she shouted to Beth. "I'll write you from California."

The five of them, Edgar, Gertie, Catherine, Grace, and Marjorie sat atop the piles of hides while the Indians propelled the boat swiftly downriver. Gertie could hardly remember a time when she had not had Beth by her side; her absence created a strangeness in their midst. When the landing was out of sight, Gertie dried her eyes and faced her future westward.

After so many months of hard travel, Gertie enjoyed the boat ride. After walking alongside oxen for so many miles, she relished watching the Indians paddled them down stream. She was disappointed they had left the lush green Walla Walla valley behind, and were once again in a near desert land. She watched the sparse juniper trees and sagebrush covered hillsides drift by.

As the boat rose and fell with the rough water, she nestled tightly beside her husband. Gertie marveled at how happy she was. It had not been her wish to leave her family in Cincinnati, and she had never wanted to travel the Oregon Trail, however, she would not have ever wished to be anywhere else than in that boat with Edgar.

Arriving at The Dalles, the small party of travelers carried their belongings among the throng of immigrants struggling to get their wagons down the narrow, muddy pathway around the Celilo Falls. Gertie watched several natives use hand-made nets and spears to fish along the edge of the riverbank. They sold their catch of salmon to the immigrants camped beside the river.

The Chinook Indians packed their boat's cargo on horse-drawn carts. The five Indians hoisted the boat on their shoulders and carried it along the footpath. On the other side of the falls, they reloaded the boat and they continued the trip down river. Along this section of the river, sheer basalt cliffs rose sharply from the banks of the river. There was not the slightest sign of a riverbank. There was no possibility of livestock or men walking along the river. Those traveling by wagon had to disassemble them and load them onto boats. Their livestock were herded along an overland trail on the slope of Mount Hood. Oxen and wagons were reunited at the Cascade Rapids, where the wagons were reassembled and driven along a narrow path around the rapids. In places, logs were laid across the muddy path to create what was known as a corduroy road; in other places, the path was a foot under water. At the bottom of the rapids, the wagons were once again disassembled and loaded on barges to take them downriver to Portland.

Departing The Dalles, Gertie, Edgar, and the others continued the boat ride through what was known as the Gorge. The powerful arms of the Indians propelled the boat past the barges drifting with the current. The flow of the water was on occasion turbulent.

"It is gorgeous," Gertie quipped, as she hung on for dear life.

"This stretch through the gorge is eight miles long. Sorry to say, but most of it is a rough ride," one Indian said. "The gorge is five miles wide and four thousand feet from the top to the water." He gestured to the rim of the cliffs high above their heads. This particular Indian had made this trip many times in the past. It was with pride that he shared his knowledge of distance and height as they progressed through the gorge.

With each mile they traversed down the river, the scenery changed dramatically from scruffy, yellowish-brown rocky hills to lofty mountain sides covered with lush emerald-green trees, shrubs and ferns. Gertie stared in awe at the magnificent sites and the grand vista she saw unfolding before her eyes. Steep, towering waterfalls tumbled down the moss-draped mountain cliffs. Mist rose from the dense arboreal canopy. Gertie had her first view of a real rainforest. Some of the trees were huge and she imagined them to be ancient, wise overseers of the forest.

Rounding one bend in the river, an enormous snowcapped mountain suddenly loomed to their left. She had seen many mountains on this journey, but none so dramatic as Mt. Hood rising sharply from the valley floor. It was almost a perfectly shaped cone. Gertie could hardly see the mountain's peak, reaching high into the wispy clouds.

The entire vista was breathtaking in its beauty. It was a visual feast, and the travelers felt satiated.

When Gertie and the others reached the Cascade Rapids, they disembarked and walked around the white, churning water. Edgar had been correct. They traveled much faster without the burden of the wagon—they had no need of it. As she had done so many times with Peter, she held one side of the trunk while Edgar held the other. Mrs. Clarke and the two girls each carried their belongings inside of a sack fashioned from spare canvas. After the mile and a half walk, they camped and ate fried salmon. The greasy fish softened the hardtack. While the meal was simple, it was hot and filling. During the chilly night, they huddled close together under the buffalo hide.

CHAPTER SEVENTEEN

September 24, 1848
Oregon City

The following morning, Edgar hired a boat to complete their journey to Oregon City. Despite their sidetrack to the Whitman Mission, they arrived ahead of the others who had been in Major Jamison's wagon train.

The small town was bursting at the seams with emigrants. After having been on the wide open prairie for such a long period of time, Gertie was mesmerized by the sight of civilization. Edgar secured a simple tent for their shelter; it was the only lodging available in the overcrowded city. Though minimal for their needs, it had a wooden floor and stove for heat, and they managed to fit five cots inside. In the morning they inquired at the Claim Office where the Sager homestead was located, and on the following day Edgar rented a horse and buggy to take Catherine to her Uncle and her new home. Along the way, Gertie admired the Willamette Valley with its green fields dotted with yellow flowers.

"It's just as I dreamed," Gertie mused.

Catherine was delighted to be with family once again; she had last seen her uncle two years earlier. However, her parting with Gertie and Edgar was filled with sadness.

"I will never forget all that you've done for me," Catherine said, her voice filled with the maturity of a young woman who had suffered much.

"We'll write to you from California," Gertie promised. "God willing, one day we will see each other again, someday."

Edgar and Gertie remained in Oregon City one more day to assist Grace as she secured a position as a clerk in a dry goods store. "He's a widower," Grace whispered, and winked. "And he has a daughter a year older than Marjorie." The position came with the use of a room over the store and Marjorie enrolled in the school. With a wink, Grace mused that she would be married before the New Year.

Gertie and Edgar each wrote letters to their parents. Gertie told her mother that she was safe in Oregon and that she had married Edgar Millar. She related very few details of her adventure on the Oregon Trail, and said nothing of what had transpired at the Whitman Mission. She finished her letter stating she was bound for San Francisco and would write again when they were settled.

The newlyweds bought tickets for the steamboat *Beaver* to take them to Astoria, further west on the Columbia River. In the port city, they secured passage on a schooner bound for San Francisco. As partial payment for their passage, Edgar helped load the ship's cargo of logs and agreed to assist as a crewmember. He told Gertie the work was not hard and it would help them get to California as cheaply as possible. She remembered the money hidden in the false bottom of her trunk and told him about it. While he was overjoyed their situation was secured, he kept the position as crewman.

The ship ventured into the Pacific Ocean. Gertie stared at the billowing, white sails and thought about her trip across the Atlantic so many years earlier. With a tear in her eye, she remembered how she had enjoyed watching the prairie schooners sail across the sea of grass in the early days of her Oregon Trail adventure. While this had been only four months earlier, it seemed to her as though it had been another lifetime.

Is this the journey's end?

She recalled her family and wished she could hug them. She stroked her cheek, summoning the memory of the tickle her father's beard left when he kissed her. The sound of her mother's voice, cautioning her to "be careful" echoed through her mind. She chuckled with the memory of her childhood, playing with her sister Ida under the watchful eyes of her brothers.

As the day ended, Edgar and Gertie were at long last alone in their tiny stateroom. While the cabin had two bunk beds, they slept together in one. Entwining naked, in passion and love, they finally consummated their marriage.

Gertie knew this was a new beginning for them and their lives would hold all the excitement she had dreamed of and feared not having. The Oregon Trail had made her a widow, but it had also given her Edgar. She couldn't be happier. As they lay together, she watched Edgar, lost in his own thoughts.

"What are thinking about, my love?" she asked.

"Oh, I was imagining how beautiful you will be pregnant with our child."

Gertie stroked her belly and wondered when that time would come. She so very much wanted his child. Life would not be easy, but they were together and she longed for the joy of their own family.

The ship gently rocked and Edgar pulled her even closer. As they continued to lie quietly in their marriage bed, Gertie imagined their future. She saw them on a hilltop looking off into the distance, standing side by side. Edgar was holding both she and their child snuggly in his arms. What awaited them? It didn't matter. Whatever the adventure may be, they would face it together...always.

The End

ABOUT THE AUTHOR

S. M. Revolinski is a retired engineer who, when he is not consulting or trading stock options, enjoys writing. While not exactly science fiction, most of his stories are connections between the supernatural and the real world – what if 'this' really happened?

With his "Widow's Trail", he has gone for pure history. This work contains much of the real life experienced by the travelers along the Oregon Trail in 1848. In those days, were only a few structures to be seen from one end to the other. This story melds together many real life accounts of this grueling adventure.

To enjoy more of these stories, look for:
Ashes Into Stardust
Torpedo Secrets
River Mermaid
A Pirate's Wife For Me
Children of the Fallen Star
Murder at Holyrood Palace
To Murder a Queen
One War at a Time
The Truth About Mermaids

FREE SAMPLE OF 'A PIRATE'S WIFE FOR ME'

Synopsis

Pirates – Romance - Adventure

As punishment for deceiving them, Anne McKinnon is taken prisoner by the pirates. "I will let you buy her back," the pirate John Rackham offers to her father. A ransom deal is struck and her father has six months to travel to England, collect the money, and return to the Bahamas to rescue is daughter. Twirling his finger in Anne's hair, the pirate snarls, "She will serve me, while I will wait for your return." Working as the pirate's cook, Anne will have to survive on her own; she has only her own wits to protect her now.

Anne knew that nothing would ever be the same when she and her father set sail from Scotland, bound for the New World. She knew that adventures awaited them on the voyage to Jamaica. However, being kidnapped, ransomed, and sold into slavery were not the adventures she had anticipated. And then, her vengeance is unleashed.

This story is one of a young woman's coming of age as she experiences the romance and tribulations of the high seas in the early 18th century.

Excerpt

Anne had been hiding as ordered. She made no sound when the pirates searched the crew's quarters or when they came into the sail locker. However, they were sufficiently experienced to know where valuables were hidden aboard ships. They tore through the sail cloths, searching every inch of the small room. As they were searching for something as small as a gold coin, they could not possibly miss something as large as a girl.

"Ah, Captain," the pirate said as he traced a finger along Anne's jaw, "it appears you have a stowaway on-board your ship."

Though his hands clenched into fists, Douglas steeled his emotions. He had seen the pirate execute the resisting passenger and he knew that Anne would be no better off with him dead.

"No, she is not a stowaway. She is a mere child, and I ordered her to be hidden. But, there still is no more money aboard."

"Whose child is she?"

Douglas knew that if he revealed that she was his daughter, they would torture her until he revealed where more valuables were hidden.

"She is just an orphan girl that I hired to cook for the passengers, and to clean up after them."

"A cook? I'm hungry. Go prepare us a meal, child. Watch her closely," the pirate captain said to the man holding Anne's hair as she was dragged from the room.

Douglas had been eager for the pirates to leave, but now they would be staying longer.

Under the supervision of two pirates, Anne prepared a meal as quickly as possible. While the food was some of the poorest she had ever prepared, the pirates devoured it as though she had cooked ambrosia. She had wished that she could have poisoned them, but she had no poison. Besides, they had demonstrated themselves to be very clever; she was afraid that they would force Papa to eat the food first.

Belching after his meal, the pirate captain said, "You are indeed a fine cook, lassie. I think you shall come with us and be our cook."

"NO! Please," Douglas injected. "I will pay you not to take her."

"Pay? With what? I have already taken all of your money, so you said."

"Here." Knowing that the pirate might make good his threat to burn the ship, Douglas risked everything to save his daughter. He opened a hidden compartment in his desk and gave five hundred pieces-of-eight to the pirate. "This is the last I have. Please, leave her be."

"Ah," the pirate captain took the coins, but ignored Douglas' request. "You do remember what I said I would do if I found more money after my final warning?"

"You didn't find it." Douglas bargained as though he were bargaining with the devil himself. "I gave it to you."

The pirate laughed, clearly enjoying the banter. "She is *your* daughter." He tilted her chin up and observing the resemblance between them.

"Aye, please don't do her any harm."

"Too bad you hid her and lied about the money. I don't appreciate being deceived. You must be punished." Douglas realized that he should have followed his own plan of complacency to the letter. "I will let you buy her back. But, she will cost much more than this." The pirate jingled the silver coins.

"I pray to God that you believe me, I have *no more money*!"

"Then you will have to get it. You may proceed along your voyage and sell your cargo. Bring me the money and I will give her back to you."

"The people of Jamaica have no money. I was going to trade my cargo of ironworks for their sugar, tobacco, and such that I could then sell in England. Only then would my cargo be converted to gold."

The pirate twirled his finger in Anne's short hair. She spat into his face. Wiping away the spittle, he said, "I am a patient man. She will serve me, while I will wait for your return."

"But! But, that will be months!"

"You best hurry then." The pirate captain pushed Anne into the arms of the two men behind her. "Take her to the ship," he barked.

"Sir, I beg you. She is an innocent." Douglas referenced Anne's unmarried status.

The two pirates pulled Anne from the room. She wished she could scream, but somehow her throat refused to open.

"Is that so?" the pirate captain snarled. "I'll give you six months to complete your voyage to Jamaica, sail to England to sell your cargo, and then return here. I will keep her in New Providence – safe and *innocent*. If you do not produce ten thousand pieces-of-eight by the end of that time, then I will sell her for what I can get *elsewhere*."

Douglas did not imagine that the cruel man would keep his word, but he had no choice. "How will I find you?"

"I am Captain John Rackham. Everyone there will know of me. Sail into New Providence under a white flag and tell the harbor master that you have business with me. You will be safe, if you present no trickery."

The men pushed Anne toward the ship's railing.

"Hey, take me with you. I want to join you and be a pirate too," a voice cried out with a Dutch accent.

Anne turned to see which of the *Matilda*'s crewmembers was turning coat, but the men were lifting her into the air by her arms. As her feet kicked under her skirt, they pushed her over the side.

"Sure, lad, come along," one of the pirates said. The traitorous crewman sprinted over the side and dropped into the boat as Anne was being lowered, still hanging by her arms.

When her feet reached the boat, she came eyeball to eyeball with the traitor, it was Mary Read. She was dressed as a man. "Keep silent and I will keep you safe," she whispered.

She could imagine no means by which the woman could keep such a promise, but Anne kept silent.

Made in United States
Orlando, FL
06 June 2025